"Don't do that, Flora."

"What? What am I doing?"

"You're treating me like the enemy again. I'm here. I'm with you." For a moment their gazes locked. "For you, not against you. I'll come with you."

Flora felt as if the ground were crumbling beneath her feet. That like the cliff face before them, the foundations upon which she lived her life were being undermined by Bram Gifford. First he had taken her hand and she had not pulled away. Too late, she'd learned that she was not immune to the touch of a man's hand, a certain look in his eyes, the hot lick of desire.

He'd kissed her with a sweetness that was designed to turn her head, make her forget that they were rivals. That they were both after the same prize.

And she'd forgotten.

Dear Reader,

Welcome to my brand-new trilogy, BOARDROOM
BRIDEGROOMS.

Claibourne & Farraday is "the most stylish department
store in London." On the retirement of their father, the
three talented Claibourne sisters are all set to take the store
into the twenty-first century. Romana as head of public
relations, Flora, a designer, and India, the oldest of the
sisters, stepping into her father's shoes as managing director.

But the Farradays, three dynamic businessmen with plans
of their own for Claibourne & Farraday, are determined to
take full control of the store back into Farraday hands.

India invites the Farraday cousins to "work-shadow"
the sisters in order to find out what it takes to run the store.
In this book, quiet reserved Flora tries to avoid being work
shadowed—only, her plan backfires, and she's now stuck
with playboy Bram Farraday Gifford on a romantic island
paradise....

With love,

Liz Fielding

To find out more about Liz Fielding, visit her Web site at
www.lizfielding.com

BOARDROOM BRIDEGROOMS!
It's a marriage takeover!

Read all three books in this exciting trilogy by Liz Fielding!
May 2002: *The Corporate Bridegroom*, HR #3700
June 2002: *The Marriage Merger*, HR #3704
July 2002: *The Tycoon's Takeover*, HR #3708

LIZ FIELDING
The Marriage Merger

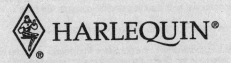

TORONTO • NEW YORK • LONDON
AMSTERDAM • PARIS • SYDNEY • HAMBURG
STOCKHOLM • ATHENS • TOKYO • MILAN • MADRID
PRAGUE • WARSAW • BUDAPEST • AUCKLAND

For Betty, Nancy, Doris, Glenys and Eiddwen…
my mother and her sisters…
with all my love

ISBN 0-373-03704-X

THE MARRIAGE MERGER

First North American Publication 2002.

Copyright © 2002 by Liz Fielding.

PROLOGUE

CITY DIARY, LONDON EVENING POST

WHAT is going on at Claibourne & Farraday?

Following the departure of Peter Claibourne last month, it's rumoured that London's most stylish department store has become a war zone, with the Claibournes and the Farradays in a battle to control the boardroom.

The two families each own forty-nine per cent of the store, with the remaining 'golden share' of two per cent passing to the oldest male heir of either family, and with it total control over the future of the company.

Peter's lovely daughters, who have been part of the store since their pictures appeared in C&F's first mail order catalogue for nursery furniture, have cited equality in the workforce and refused to move over. I am informed that, confident of their position, they have invited the Farradays to 'shadow' them during the next few months, promising to step down if the men can do a better job.

Today's surprise announcement of the marriage of Romana Claibourne, youngest of the Claibourne girls, to Niall Farraday Macaulay in a brief ceremony in Las Vegas would suggest one Farraday was so impressed with the woman he was shadowing that he married her.

With Bram Farraday Gifford about to take his turn shadowing jewellery buyer and designer Flora Claibourne, we await the outcome with considerable interest. Watch this space.

MEMORANDUM
From: J D FARRADAY
To: BRAM FARRADAY GIFFORD
Subject: CLAIBOURNE & FARRADAY

Bram, the Claibourne girls are playing dirty. If Romana Claibourne was able to subvert Niall to their cause, she must be a lot cleverer than she looks. Flora Claibourne, as you will see from the file I'm biking over to you, just looks clever.

Since the gloves are now off, I see no reason why you shouldn't employ your infamous charm to even the score.

E-MAIL
From: Dr T Myan, Minister of Antiquities, Saraminda
To: Flora Claibourne, London

My dear Miss Claibourne

You will no doubt have seen sensational reports of the discovery of a rich burial site in Saraminda. As you can guess, we have been overwhelmed with requests from journalists wishing to view this 'lost princess', as they have dubbed her.

As a matter of urgency my government has asked me to approach you, as an authority on ancient jewellery and the author of *Ashanti Gold*, to write about the treasure. Your combination of scholarship and vivid writing would put this truly extraordinary find above lurid exploitation.

I would be grateful if you could respond by return.

Your honoured friend
Tipi Myan

FAX
From: INDIA CLAIBOURNE
To: BRAM GIFFORD
Subject: WORK SHADOWING

Miss Flora Claibourne will be travelling to Saraminda on Wednesday 1st May on a work-related project. Since you will be shadowing her during that month I have made arrangements for you to travel with her. I attach an itinerary for your information.

A car will collect you and deliver you to the airport in good time for the flight. Should you have any queries, please call this office.

CHAPTER ONE

'SARAMINDA?' Bram Gifford took the fax from his secretary. 'Isn't that some island in the middle of nowhere? One plane a week in the dry season if the pilot's sober?'

'Not so. I checked it out on the Internet. Saraminda, according to the sales pitch, is an undiscovered paradise. It's being touted as the latest luxury "fall off the end of the earth" holiday destination.'

'Paradise is overrated. It inevitably comes with a serpent.' He knew that for a fact. He'd got the scars to prove it. 'Besides, this isn't luxury, this is a package tour,' he said as he scanned the fax. 'Flora Claibourne is the package.' Then, 'What "work-related project" could involve a couple of weeks in this doubtful paradise, do you suppose?'

'Maybe the Claibourne girls are looking into the possibility of opening a local branch to sell designer swimsuits and sun specs to rich tourists?'

Bram pulled a face. 'Please let it be so. That level of incompetence would be a gift.'

'But unlikely. Nothing I've ever heard about the Claibourne girls suggests they're incompetent. It's more likely that Flora's going to have a look at this "lost princess" they've found in some ruins deep in the interior. Dripping with gold and jade and pearls and goodness knows what else.' She handed him a printout from the tourist department website. 'Flora Claibourne designs the most stunning jewellery exclusively for the store.'

'So?'

'Maybe she's looking for inspiration.'

He tossed the paper on his desk. 'More likely it's some fancy way of keeping me out of the way while their lawyers waste their time searching for some way to prevent us from ousting them.'

'Maybe it is, but you'll be shadowing her anyway and it has to beat trailing her around a department store for a month. You could do with a holiday.'

'This won't be a holiday.'

'I'm sure it won't be as bad as you think. You've got a lot in common.'

'We both have a major holding in a department store. And we both want to be in control,' he agreed, with just a touch of irony. 'Whether that will make for a relaxing time, I take leave to doubt.'

'Is she pretty? Her sisters are lovely but I don't think I've ever seen a photograph of Flora.'

Bram offered her a copy of *Ashanti Gold*, the latest non-fiction title to grip the public imagination and become a runaway bestseller. 'Her picture's on the back,' he said, leaving her to make up her own mind.

'Oh, well, I suppose you can't have everything. You'll be in paradise; getting Eve would be too much to ask. You'll just have to lie back, close your eyes and remember how much you want to get your hands on that department store.'

'Haven't you got something important to do?' he asked irritably.

'Yes, but this is more interesting. I'll go and make some coffee.'

Left to himself, Bram took out his wallet. At the back, stashed away where no one would see, was a snapshot of a small boy with his puppy. He looked at it for a long time. Then, about to return it to its hiding place, he put it instead in the small pocket provided for such treasures.

It was a timely reminder that he'd thought he'd found paradise once, when he was young enough to believe in such a concept. He'd bitten the apple and found the serpent.

'You've done what?'

'Don't look at me like that, Flora Claibourne. You were there when it was arranged for Bram Gifford to shadow you during May. I asked you to put off your trip, but you went ahead and arranged it anyway.'

It had been a matter of self-preservation. Flora didn't think her sister would accept that as an excuse, however, so she pleaded a higher cause. 'I can't put off an invitation from the Saramindan government until it's more convenient for you, India. You might be pretty big here, but I don't suppose they've ever heard of Claibourne & Farraday.'

'Nonsense. Their royal family has an account with us.' She shrugged. 'But it doesn't matter. If you won't stay here and let Mr Gifford watch you at work, he must go with you to Saraminda.'

'That's out of the question.' Flora reached up to capture a handful of untidy curls that had slithered from a comb, twisting them carelessly into a knot on top of her head and anchoring them out of her eyes. 'And pointless. I don't know a thing about running Claibourne & Farraday, Indie. I just design the occasional jewellery collection—'

India regarded her younger sister with undisguised exasperation. 'You do a lot more than that,' she said. 'I don't think you understand just how important you are to us. You bring us your own amazing jewellery designs, new fabrics you've picked up on your travels, and before you know it the entire store has been inspired. Last year you went to Africa and this summer everyone's going to be wearing hot colours and animal prints to go with those gold wire chokers and cuffs. The opposition is scrambling to catch up. But you know what they say about a bandwagon. If you can see it—'

'You've missed it. I know.'

'And this autumn and winter is going to be fabulous. Celtic silver and platinum jewellery against soft, misty greens and mauves...'

Flora knew when she was being buttered up, and this was buttering on a grand scale. 'Indie—'

'Enough. You didn't object at the time, and one month out of your life is not a lot to ask...' she paused briefly '...considering you're a director of this company.'

'That was not my choice. I'm not a businesswoman.' She'd been railroaded into taking it on in order to show solidarity against the Farradays. 'I really don't have the time—'

'I'll let you go, Flora—and I promise I'll never ask you to do another thing for me once this Farraday

nonsense is out of the way—but I need you to show
total commitment right now. Not next month. Not next
year. Now. We have to offer a united front in the face
of their attempt to grab control. Please don't be difficult.'

Flora wanted to be difficult. She wanted to scream
and stamp and throw things, just the way her mother
did when she didn't get her way. Knowing from experience just how unattractive that was, she restrained
herself. She didn't give up, though. 'I'm going there
to look at some ancient finery, take some pictures and
then write about it, Indie. It's not a spectator sport,'
she said. 'And Bram Gifford will not be amused when
he finds out that it's nothing to do with the store.'

'You'll have to convince him that it is. Tell him
you're working on next year's collection. Ask his advice about camera angles if he gets tricky,' she
suggested, abandoning buttering in favour of arm-
twisting. 'Men can't resist any opportunity to display
their superiority. Especially Farraday men,' she added,
with feeling. 'I just need you to keep Bram Gifford
busy and out of my hair while the lawyers work on a
strategy to keep them out. It isn't much to ask.' She
paused only long enough to draw breath. 'Unless you
want to see them move in and take over?'

Flora didn't care much one way or the other, but
she knew better than to say so.

'The last thing I want is him being left to his own
devices, poking around the store, probing into things
that don't concern him,' India added. 'And if you
leave him behind, that's what he'll be doing.'

Flora thought that as a major shareholder Abraham

Farraday Gifford had every right to ask difficult questions. But since that was part of the agreement—whichever family was in control ran the place without interference—she didn't bother to say so. Her apparently watertight excuse to avoid getting involved in this shadowing scheme had just developed a leak.

'Any progress with the lawyers?' she asked, infinitely hopeful.

'Well, the fact that the agreement states control should pass to the ''oldest male heir'' offers considerable scope on the sex discrimination front, but it isn't going to hold Jordan Farraday for long. He's older than I am, so he can surrender the ''male'' bit without giving away a thing—'

'After which it'll be a mad race to see who can produce the first baby Claibourne or Farraday so that the next generation can do this again in another thirty years,' said Flora. Put like that, maybe she did have a duty to help put an end to such nonsense.

Her sister apparently missed the irony, because she simply shrugged and said, 'As women, I think we might have the upper hand there.'

Flora doubted that. She strongly suspected that if Bram Gifford called for volunteers, he'd be in severe danger of being trampled in the crush.

'In the meantime,' she went on, 'I've got to make my case on the grounds of equality in the workplace. Which means proving I'm Jordan Farraday's equal.'

'So prove it. Go ahead and announce your stunning plans for the total revamping of Claibourne & Farraday. Surely that's the quickest way to demonstrate your capability?'

'There's a problem with that.'

Flora waited.

'I can't announce my plans right now because they include removing the name Farraday from the store.'

'What?'

'I'm going to relaunch it as Claibourne's. One snappy, modern name instead of two long-winded ones.'

'Oh, fudge! I really wish you hadn't told me that.' Flora really wished she hadn't asked. She wasn't good at secrets. Not those kind of secrets. She'd used up her entire store of secrecy genes keeping just one. 'I can see how that might be…um…'

'Like waving a red rag at a bull? Inviting court injunctions and goodness knows what else?'

'I shouldn't think goodness would have much to do with it.'

'Which is why you have to keep Bram Gifford occupied for the next month. Try and stun him with one of your flashes of genius—demonstrate just how indispensable you are to the success of the store. I don't expect him to be on our side, but if he can be neutralised—'

'You're not suggesting I neutralise him the way Romana neutralised Niall?' Flora asked. 'Because I'm telling you now—'

'Until they return from their honeymoon we won't know who neutralised whom,' she said. 'I need you, Flora. I really need you.'

That her sister would admit to needing anyone had to be a first. India had always been entirely self-sufficient. But Flora had her own problems. 'I just don't see what I can do. I'm going to be working in the museum most of the time and when I'm not there I'm going to have to take a trip into the interior to look at the excavations. It'll be very short on mod cons and it's got nothing to do with the store.' She hoped, if she kept repeating that, India might eventually realise the futility of involving her.

'Bram Gifford doesn't have to know that.'

'Oh, please! His middle name is Farraday. He won't be that easy to fool.'

'Then don't even try. The Tutankhamun treasure inspired the Egyptian look. With a bit of effort your "lost princess" could do the same. Just give us something to work with. And it won't hurt Mr Gifford to work up a sweat following you through the rainforest.'

'What about me?'

'You won't even notice the discomfort. You never do.' India finally smiled. 'It won't be that bad, Flora. I've been doing a little research of my own and, believe me, Bram Gifford is at the top of every girl's wish list.'

'Not mine,' she said, with feeling. She'd seen photographs of him in *Celebrity* magazine—a golden bear of a man, oozing wealth and power, with an endless succession of lovely women clinging to his arm.

Her mother would adore him.

'Hey, I'm not suggesting anything serious, but it wouldn't hurt to flirt with him a little. Just don't, whatever you do, fall in love with the man.'

The warning was quite unnecessary. If he was going to be dogging her heels, the next month was going to be quite bad enough without making a total fool of herself. Once was more than enough. But she didn't say that. What she said was, 'Don't be silly. There isn't a girl alive who could meet him without falling in love with him. That's what men like Bram Gifford are *for*.' Her mother had an entire collection of them. But she pulled a face so that India would know she was joking.

India, realising that she'd won, laughed more with relief than amusement. 'I have the feeling that meeting you will be a unique experience for him.'

Bram leafed through the thick file of newspaper cuttings and magazine articles that in one way or another touched on the life of Flora Claibourne. Other than the dreary formal portrait used on the jacket of her book, which made her look ten years older that she was, and the broadsheet reviews, few concerned her as an individual.

Mostly they included her as an add-on. She was a member of a well-known family whose loves and lives had always provided fodder for newspaper diarists. She didn't appear to have had any affairs worth reporting, though. Unlike her mother, who was a tabloid editor's dream.

Peter Claibourne's second wife had been a model. Tall, leggy and stunningly good-looking in those early photographs. She hadn't stayed with Claibourne long. She hadn't stayed with anyone long. She must be in her forties now, although cosmetic surgery and kind lighting made her appear closer to Flora's age. Maybe that was why they had rarely been seen together much once Flora had grown out of photogenic babyhood.

The myth of endless youth would not survive the comparison, and since her latest husband—formerly her personal trainer—was considerably younger than her, that illusion was a necessity.

And Flora might prefer it that way too. It must be tough to be compared with your mother and found wanting.

On those rare occasions on which she'd been forced to put on a long frock and makeup she looked ill at ease, as if desperate to escape and return to the safety of her books. She looked, he decided, like a virgin who didn't quite know what her body was for.

An innocent little fish just waiting for a cunningly tied fly to be drifted temptingly over the water? It seemed unlikely. She was twenty-six years old. There must be more to her than that.

There was a long ring at the doorbell.

He took one last look at the photograph. It was true that she was no Eve, but it was entirely possible she'd open up like a flower to the sun in response to a little attention. He wouldn't be closing his eyes, though. He'd be watching her every minute of the day.

Picking up the overnight bag that contained his passport, along with the essentials for coping with a long flight, he went to answer it.

'Mr Gifford? Your car for the airport, sir.'

Flora Claibourne barely looked up from the notes she was reading as he joined her in the rear of the limousine that was taking them to the airport. Just long enough to nod and say, 'I'm sorry about dragging you away like this, Mr Gifford. I hope I haven't inconvenienced you.'

She was wearing a crumpled linen trouser suit in some indescribably drab colour, her hair an untidy bird's nest inadequately secured with pins and combs. If she'd tried, he thought, she couldn't have looked less appealing.

He turned on a suitably low-wattage smile to match her cool businesslike manner. Maybe the sun would warm her up.

'It's Bram,' he said. 'And don't apologise. A couple of weeks on a tropical island sounds a lot more attractive than following you around a department store.'

'The whole purpose of this exercise is to demonstrate what it takes to run a department store,' she pointed out, not bothering with a smile of any kind. Or a return invitation to use her given name.

Prickly, as well as plain. God, he hated women who made no attempt to look attractive, instead challenging the male of the species to hunt for inner beauty and gain his true reward. He had news for her. The average male wasn't interested in inner beauty. But it wasn't his job to tell her that. His brief was to find out what was going on behind the scenes at Claibourne & Farraday.

He didn't think flattery would impress her much either, so he said, 'If that were the case we'd both be wasting our time. You know nothing and since I'm a lawyer, not a shopkeeper, I'm not especially interested.'

The smile hadn't made any impression; maybe he could disarm her with frankness. Okay, so he wasn't being totally frank. He was very interested in getting the Claibournes out and the Farradays in with the min-imum amount of fuss. Legally.

'At least this way I'll be wasting my time in the sun.'

She glanced at him again without raising her head, just a sideways look—a lift of lashes untroubled by mascara but long and dark enough without it. In any other woman he'd have taken it as the opening move in a game of flirtation, but Flora appeared to be totally oblivious of the effect such a look might provoke. Or maybe she was cleverer than he'd given her credit for. She must have learned something from her mother, even if she'd only absorbed it by osmosis.

'Have you packed walking boots?' she asked.

No, she was oblivious, he decided.

'Should I have?'

She shrugged, as if it was of no particular concern to her whether he had or not. 'I anticipate taking a trip into the interior. It might be rough going. Of course you don't have to come with me.' She reached up and pushed a comb more firmly into the bird's nest. 'I'm sure you'd be much happier staying at the beach.'

Roughly translated, that meant, *I'd* be much happier if you stayed on the beach, he thought. She'd probably be a lot happier if he stayed at home. Well, it wasn't his role in life to make her happy.

'On the contrary, Miss Claibourne, I'm along for the ride. Wherever it goes. I'll be most interested in everything you do.'

She looked doubtful, but didn't argue, returning to the handwritten notes in the file she was holding, sug-

gesting without words that they were far more interesting that anything he might have to say.

Again, in any other woman he would have assumed
it was all part of the game and been amused, but it
was clear that Flora Claibourne didn't play games. She
really didn't care.

Round one to her, then.

His presence ignored, he opened his briefcase and
extracted a brand-new hardback book. *Ashanti Gold*,
by Flora Claibourne.

He, too, began to read.

Flora didn't miss his attempt to flatter, although why
he would bother at all surprised her. Not that it mattered, because she wasn't impressed. She'd seen all
the moves before.

He pushed long, elegant fingers through his shaggy
mane of sun-streaked hair, taking it back from his
forehead in an unconsciously graceful gesture.

That one was a classic, she thought. And beautifully
done, with not a hint of the self-conscious. He made
it look like a gesture he'd used all his life—not one
he'd practised in front of a mirror.

She still wasn't impressed. Bram Gifford might consider himself a world-class charmer, but it would take
more than the purchase of her book, a *faux* interest in
her subject, to turn her head. But she didn't say anything.

While he was pretending fascination with the history and uses of gold in West Africa he wasn't at-
tempting to engage her in conversation, which was just
fine with her.

With any luck he'd read all the way to Saraminda.

*   *   *

Saraminda. The name had an exotic ring to it and the
island didn't disappoint, Flora decided, as the small
inter-island plane banked steeply to line up with the
floor of a tropical valley, offering them a breathtaking
view of the mountainous landscape.

The lower slopes were farmed on terraces painstak-
ingly cut into the hills, but above the farms the foot-
hills rose in wave after wave, until they soared into
peaks densely thicketed with the dark green vegetation
of a rainforest that until recently had hidden the ruins
of a temple where a young woman had been buried
with all the ceremony of a queen.

Allegedly.

She'd met Tipi Myan briefly at a reception given
by the travel department at the store more than a year
ago. He hadn't been Minister of Antiquities then. He'd
been running the country's tourist authority.

Call her cynical, but if she'd been in his shoes she
might have been tempted to use that very tenuous acquaintance to ask the author of *Ashanti Gold* to write
about his "lost princess". It would provoke a lot more
interest in his island than an article by some jobbing
photo-journalist looking for a story to sell.

It had been his good fortune that she'd been looking
for an escape route at the time. One that had backfired
on her. As Bram Gifford leaned across her to get a
better look, his thick corn-coloured hair catching the
sun, the small inner voice that warned her she was
being used, grew louder.

She was being used by everyone. All that had

changed was her ability to see the game for what it was and ensure that she wasn't hurt in the process.

'We're going up there?' Bram asked, looking up at mountain peaks gold-misted in the dawn light before turning to her. He was, she thought, heart-meltingly handsome, with warm, toffee-brown eyes that crinkled at the corners when he smiled. 'You aren't bothered about snakes and spiders and creepy-crawlies?'

For pity's sake! Did she look like a bird-witted fool? Patronising cancelled out toffee-brown eyes—however crinkly their corners—every time.

'In my experience they have more reason to be scared of me than I have of them,' she replied matter-of-factly. She'd witnessed the most practised flirts at work, but she'd only been caught once. She was a quick learner, and it would take a lot more than 'Me Tarzan, you Jane' to impress her. 'There are far more unpleasant things in this world than *arthropoda*,' she added.

Bram, who'd expected the usual shiver of horror, gave a mental nod in her direction. Not too many women of his acquaintance would have resisted the opportunity to squeal a little, just to boost his 'big strong man' quotient. Or used *arthropoda* in a sentence. But then he was the first to admit that he wasn't interested in their IQ.

Having neatly put him down, she wasn't waiting for him to compliment her on her backbone either. He was getting the message, loud and clear, that she didn't care what he thought.

Instead she began gathering her personal possessions without any fuss, not taking the slightest bit of notice of him.

In his experience this was usually a calculated ploy. Not noticing men had been raised to an art form by a certain type of woman. The kind who wanted to be noticed.

He had to concede that she didn't appear to be one of them, but he'd reserve judgement.

Right now the early-morning sun, pouring in through the window, was lighting up her tortured hair and glinting off a dozen hairpins. Someone should do her a favour and throw them away, he thought. And those damned combs that she was forever replacing without seeming to notice what she was doing. As if reading his mind, she raised her hands to capture a loose strand of hair and anchor it in place.

Then, as if sensing him watching her, she let her hands drop to her lap. 'I'm so sorry, I wasn't thinking. That's so remiss of me. Are you concerned for your own safety, Mr Gifford?'

This was the nearest they'd come to a conversation in the endless hours of flying. She was still sticking to his surname though, despite his request that she call him Bram. But at least it was a question: a mocking one, to be sure, but one that required an answer. A decided advance on the monosyllabic responses she'd stuck to throughout the long flight.

Clearly a seasoned traveller, she'd eaten little, refused anything but water to drink and slept without fuss when she wasn't working—although that hadn't been often. And while they'd waited for their transfer to the Saraminda flight at Singapore she'd toured the shops, looking at everything but buying nothing. And saying even less.

He'd used the time when she'd been sleeping to take a long hard look at Flora Claibourne. She might be clever, but she was a woman, and they all had their weak spots. If he was going to get her to open up to him, trust him, confide in him, he'd have to discover hers.

Of the three Claibourne sisters she most favoured her father in looks. Not much of a start for a girl. On her, the nose only just missed being a disaster. But then all her features were larger than life. She had a full, generous mouth that might have been dangerous if she'd bothered to make the most of it. And eyes that, although a rather undistinguished shade of brown, were strikingly framed by long lashes and fine brows.

It was a face full of character, he decided. Then had recalled his formidable grandmother ticking him off when, as a callow youth, he'd rather unkindly dismissed some girl as plain. 'Her face may not be pretty, but it has character, Bram,' she'd told him. 'And she has lovely skin. That will last long after chocolate-box prettiness has lost its charm.'

He hadn't been convinced at the time. Still wasn't. But he had to admit that Flora Claibourne had lovely skin too. In the clear, unforgiving light at thirty thousand feet it had seemed almost translucent, with just the faintest dusting of freckles that had been invisible in the grey London morning they'd left behind them. The kind of skin that without sun block would frazzle to a red, peeling crisp. He hoped she didn't take her reverse vanity that far.

He'd noticed, too, that asleep she lost the wary look that she disguised well beneath a faintly aggressive attitude. So what, exactly, was she wary of? Him? He hadn't done anything to warrant wariness. Yet.

Awake, she'd concentrated on work, and he'd known better than to push his company on her. Instead he'd read her book from cover to cover, which was why he now knew more than he'd ever wanted to know about the history of gold working in West Africa. That wasn't a complaint. She had a lively style and could tell a story. It was just that he hadn't anticipated reading it all in one go.

To sum up, then, she was aggressively dowdy, wary and clever. In short, everything he disliked in a woman.

She was also, having ignored his presence for most of the flight, now taking the opportunity to poke a little fun at him. She might not have the style of her sisters, but he was beginning to suspect that she wasn't going to be the push-over he'd anticipated.

A flicker of anticipation rippled through him. An unexpected charge of excitement. It was a long time since the outcome of the chase had seemed so uncertain. Or the stakes so high.

CHAPTER TWO

'WELL?' she prompted, still waiting for his answer. 'Are you scared?'

'Of spiders? Absolutely terrified of the little beggars,' he said, the long pause lending authenticity to his apparently reluctant confession. Acknowledging a weakness had, in his experience, never failed to bring out that innate protective instinct that was the birthright of every woman.

Why spoil such a perfect opportunity to evoke her sympathy by telling the truth?

Flora regarded him levelly for a moment, as if deciding whether or not to believe him. Then she said, 'The plane has come to a stop, Mr Gifford.' He still didn't know what she thought. About anything. It was disconcerting, to say the least, and he turned away to peer out of the opposite window at quaint wooden airport buildings that were smothered with flowering climbers.

'I do believe you're right, Miss Claibourne,' he replied, getting to his feet to retrieve their bags and jackets from the overhead locker.

There was a bump as the door was opened and the aircraft was flooded with soft warm air, the smell of aircraft fuel mingling with the scent of the tropics. Musty, spicy, different.

'This certainly beats London on a grey day in May,'

he said as they walked across the tarmac towards the terminal building.

'There are no snakes in London,' she said, automatically rescuing a comb and tucking it back in place. 'Outside of the zoo. Or poisonous spiders.' She knew he'd been lying. Or at least suspected as much.

'There's always a downside. You can't have everything.'

'No, you can't, Mr Gifford.' The customs officer waved them through with a smile. 'You, for instance, can't have Claibourne's.'

Taken by surprise at her unexpected mention of the dispute, he was still groping for an appropriate answer when a short slender man, formally attired in a long silk high-necked jacket and a traditional sarong that covered him to his ankles, approached Flora and bowed politely before extending his hand.

'Miss Claibourne! What a pleasure to meet you again. And how kind of you to come so far to write about our small treasure.'

'Not at all, Dr Myan. I'd seen reports in the press and I'm excited at the prospect of seeing what you've found for myself. May I introduce my colleague, Bram Gifford?'

'Mr Gifford.' He covered his surprise with a small bow. 'Are you an expert in the same field as Miss Claibourne?'

'No,' he said. 'By "colleague" Miss Claibourne was referring to other interests we have in common.'

'Oh?' Then, with a bland look that didn't entirely hide a touch of pique, he drew his own conclusion as to what that might be. 'Oh, I see. Well, I'm sure you'll enjoy your stay, Mr Gifford. Maybe we can arrange some excursions for you while Miss Claibourne is working,' he added. 'Saraminda is a lovely country. Wonderfully peaceful,' he stressed.

'Peace and love. I'm all for it,' he said.

The flash of annoyance that had crossed Flora's face at the man's unspoken assumption that 'colleague' in this instance meant 'lover'—and his implicit response—was the first unconsidered reaction he'd got from her. He didn't give her a chance to clarify the situation.

'But I'll give the excursions a miss, thanks all the same. I'll be sticking close to Flora.' A man would hardly call his 'colleague' Miss Claibourne, now, would he? 'Whatever she does.'

Dr Myan said nothing, but his silence was eloquent. Did he fancy her himself? Bram wondered as he turned away and ushered Flora in the direction of a long black car with official numberplates, leaving him to follow in their wake with the porter.

It seemed unlikely. She was six inches taller and didn't dress to turn heads. Maybe it was her mind he admired. Or maybe he'd expected her undivided attention and was peeved that she wasn't quite as single-mindedly interested in his affairs as he'd hoped.

If that was the case, the ride in from the airport should have reassured him. She spent the journey bombarding the man with questions about the items that had been found—keen to know when she could go up into the mountains to visit the site where they had been excavated, eager to take photographs for the article she was writing.

'You wish to see the tomb?' he enquired. 'But why? There's nothing there.'

'Even so, I think I should see it.'

'It's a difficult journey, Miss Claibourne. Hard even for a man,' he said, which Bram thought was probably a mistake. 'A long walk up into the mountains. Besides, it isn't necessary,' he reiterated. 'The treasure is all at the museum.'

'But you asked if I wanted to see it,' she reminded him. 'And I do need to look at the excavations, perhaps link decoration of the tomb with the designs of the jewellery.'

'I'm sorry.' His expression was that of deep regret. 'It is not possible.'

'Not possible?' she asked. 'Why?'

Maybe Saramindan women didn't ask questions. Dr Myan clearly assumed his word would be sufficient. He wasn't prepared to offer explanations and for a moment floundered. 'The tremor…there was more damage than we first thought. We cannot take the risk,' he said, like a man clutching at passing straws.

'Are you taking steps to stabilise the structure?' Bram asked.

'Plans are being made. Engineers are being consulted,' he said carefully, as if weighing every word before uttering it. Flora glared at him for giving Tipi Myan a chance to evade her persistent questions. 'And we will restore everything so that visitors will see it as it should be seen. When it's safe. We are already making plans to build a lodge nearby for visitors, in traditional style, so that when they have seen the tomb they will be able to enjoy the ambience of a tropical forest in complete comfort.'

'If the climb up there doesn't kill them,' Flora muttered.

'You're going for the eco-tourist market?' Bram asked.

'We have many beautiful flowers, butterflies—'

Flora had had enough. 'That is very interesting, Dr Myan, but I must have photographs of the tomb for my article,' she persisted.

Bram reached out and took her hand to distract her. She turned to him with a frown. He said nothing, but she got the message just the same. She wasn't going to get anywhere by pestering Dr Myan. She retrieved her hand without fuss and let the subject drop.

'Ah, we have arrived.' And, having delivered them safely to a new luxury resort complex, the man excused himself with almost indecent haste, claiming an urgent appointment. 'I will return after the holiday. Rest, enjoy yourselves. This is a charming resort.'

'Holiday? What holiday?'

'It is a religious feast day tomorrow.'

'Holiday,' she repeated with disgust, when he'd gone. 'I've flown halfway round the world to see a tomb that is apparently out of bounds and now I'm told to sit and twiddle my thumbs while everything stops for a holiday. What on earth am I going to do tomorrow?' she demanded.

Bram could think of a dozen things. However, since she was clearly outraged at having travelled so far to the see all the riches of Saraminda only to be kept waiting, he thought it wiser not to suggest sunbathing or sightseeing as an alternative.

Instead he dealt with the formalities at Reception before they were led through the gardens to a traditional bungalow set in a garden that ran down to the beach.

Built of local timber and beautifully thatched, with a wide veranda facing the sea to catch the breeze, the single-storey, self-contained cottage offered the perfect image of a tropical holiday paradise.

He hadn't realised an academic author warranted such red carpet treatment. Of course it was just possible that the tourist authority wanted Flora Claibourne to see what was on offer, hoping she'd go home and tell her equally wealthy friends.

They were, he thought, doomed to disappointment. Beyond a request that the air conditioner be turned off, Flora appeared as oblivious to her surroundings as she was to her appearance. She was far more interested in the photographs that Tipi Myan had left with her—none of them of the tomb—than in the simple luxury of their accommodation.

Of course it was always possible that Claibourne & Farraday had booked the accommodation when they'd organised his ticket. Maybe that was why they had one of the larger bungalows with two bedrooms, since the Minister of Antiquities had quite obviously not been expecting him. Hadn't been particularly pleased to see him. Maybe Dr Myan thought he'd distract the lady from her work.

He needn't have worried. Bram thought he'd never seen anyone so focused.

'Breakfast, Flora?' he prompted, when she didn't seem to hear the hotel porter's question.

She frowned at him, irritated by the interruption or perhaps by the use of her name. 'What?' Then, registering his question, 'Oh, no.' She found a smile for the young man waiting anxiously to please her. 'Just some tea. Thank you,' she said, before returning to the photographs.

It had been the interruption, then. Pity. For a minute there he'd thought he'd got her attention. Apparently that was reserved for hammered gold. Very old hammered gold.

He picked up one of the large glossy prints, a photograph of a small, exquisitely chased cup. 'Is this what all the fuss is about?'

'It's not a fuss.' She took the photograph away from him, looked at it for a moment. 'If the finds are genuine...' She trailed off, distracted by a detail.

'If?' he prompted. She seemed taken aback by his question. 'You said *If* the finds are genuine...'

'Did I? I must be more careful not to do my thinking out loud. Dr Myan would be deeply offended at any suggestion of doubt.'

'But?'

She looked again at the photograph before returning it to the pile. 'But I wouldn't commit myself on the strength of some photographs. No matter how good. And not without seeing the site of the excavation.'

'Why would you need to see it? You're an expert in jewellery, not archaeology.'

'They want my name on an article in a leading British newspaper. For that I need more than pretty pictures of treasure. I need background.' She did some business with her hair, combing up loose strands and tucking them out of the way, then, 'You stopped me from pushing that. Why?'

The combs were a prop, he realised with a belated flash of insight. She used them as a defence mechanism, lifting her arms to fiddle with them, putting a barrier between them, cutting off eye contact. As if embarrassed that she'd questioned him so directly.

She wasn't anywhere near as cool as she would have him believe. In fact she was as nervous as a kitten.

Of him?

He'd done nothing to provoke such a reaction.

'The subject appeared to make him uncomfortable,' he said at last.

'I wonder why?'

For a moment it seemed that they were both having the same thought. That Dr Myan had something to hide. Then she retreated from their silent complicity, returning to the photographs like a snail ducking into its shell.

'I just can't believe I'm going to have to waste two days before I get a chance to look at this for myself,' she declared, with sufficient vigour to suggest her nervousness had nothing to do with him. But he suspended judgement. Flora Claibourne was a lot more complex than he'd expected.

'It doesn't have to be a waste of time,' he pointed out. 'I'm sure there's more to the island than a mysterious tomb. That beach looks inviting, for a start. I hope you packed a swimsuit along with your walking boots.'

She looked up at him, then turned quickly away to look out across the garden. 'It never occurred to me,' she said. 'But don't let me stop you enjoying yourself.' She opened her laptop, switched it on and plugged it into a telephone point.

About to suggest that she'd be wiser putting her feet up, taking a nap, he thought better of it. Patronising her was not going to make him Mr Popularity, and so, leaving her to it, he went in search of his bag. It was set alongside Flora's in a large, airy bedroom with a steeply pitched raftered ceiling.

There was a total absence of clutter that he found pleasing. Just acres of dark, polished wooden floor broken only by blue and gold native rugs. There was nothing else to distract from the four-poster bed. Draped in sheer creamy cloth that stirred in the faint breeze, it was very picturesque. Very inviting.

Somehow he didn't think Flora would be amenable to taking his declared intention to stick close to her '...whatever she did...' that literally, no matter what Dr Myan might be thinking. Retrieving his bag, he moved on to the next room, which was almost identical, with a luxurious bathroom and a large walk-in wardrobe. All it lacked was a warm and eager woman to share the long tropical nights with him.

What he'd got was Flora.

It was just as well that enjoyment was the last thing on his mind right now. He felt as if he'd been travelling for ever. He wanted a shower and then he wanted to sleep. That bed looked mighty inviting.

But he knew that beating jet lag was best served by keeping local hours, and so, virtuously ignoring the siren lure of clean white linen, he took a long, cool, wake-up shower.

Flora tapped in the password to her laptop, her eyes more interested in the back view of Bram Gifford disappearing in the direction of the bedrooms.

What on earth was the man playing at? Okay, the Claibourne & Farraday thing wasn't anyone's business but their own, but he'd as good as implied that they were lovers. Tipi Myan had certainly thought so.

What had *she* been playing at, doing nothing to correct that impression?

She rubbed her hands over her face in an attempt to keep herself awake. At the time it had seemed too complicated to explain—at least that was what she'd told herself. Too complicated and none of Tipi Myan's business.

She frowned. Despite the man's fawning welcome, it was clear that something had happened since she'd spoken to him on the phone and agreed to write the article.

She found herself clenching the hand that Bram had taken in silent warning, reliving the moment when their minds had had but one single thought. It had made them—for a heartbeat—partners, allies, on the same side against the world.

She rubbed her palm over her fist, as if to eradicate the memory of his touch. It had been too familiar. Everything about him was too familiar. As was her reaction to him. But then women always fell in love with the same man, over and over again. They never learned, so it was said.

Perhaps she was smarter than most women. Or maybe her lesson had been harder taught. Because she'd put up her defences and now neither her famous name nor her money was sufficient inducement to tempt a man to look in her direction twice. And, if he did, it simply proved he had ulterior motives. A lose-lose situation for any man who bothered.

Bram Gifford was different, though. He didn't want her money: he had more than enough to last several lifetimes. Nor did he seek the cachet of her famous name. He had his own, right there between the Bram and the Gifford. He was a Farraday to his fingertips.

He only wanted one thing from her. To discover her weaknesses and use them against her and her family.

With her mind quite straight on that point, she reached for her keyboard, setting the search engine to hunt for any reference to Saraminda, hoping to find some clue as to what on earth was going on.

Bram felt almost human. All he needed was coffee and food and he'd make it through the day.

Probably.

He dressed quickly in a pair of comfortable shorts and a faded T-shirt that had been washed duster-soft. Then he padded barefoot out onto the veranda and stretched out on a cane armchair, where the waiter found him when he brought him a light breakfast.

He signed the chit and thanked the young man, who continued to hover a little anxiously. 'Sir,' he said. 'Sir—madam is sleeping.'

She'd finally wound down and gone for a nap, had she? He was relieved to hear it. She must have been running on empty. He'd done that in the past, just kept going, his body clock all over the place, his brain running on pure adrenalin. There was always a payback.

'Don't worry. She'll have tea later.'

'No, sir. Madam sleeps in her chair.' He crossed his arms and lowered his head on them in a mime to show exactly how she'd gone to sleep, with her head on her arms at the desk.

'Oh, I see.' Not so good. He'd done that too, and he knew from experience that when she woke it would be with muscles screaming and her neck in urgent need of an osteopath. 'I'll take care of it.'

He walked along the veranda to the living room and paused in the doorway, grinning despite himself. She must have crashed out over the keyboard not long after he'd left her. The laptop was switched on. It was still connected to the Internet: her head was pressed against the keyboard and the screen was going crazy.

He touched her shoulder lightly. She didn't stir. He gave it a little shake. She grumbled and turned her head away from him so that he could see the imprint of the keys at her temple. And carried on sleeping.

Her mind, after running almost continually for twenty-four hours, had finally shut down on her.

He didn't blame it.

He closed the Internet connection, switched off the laptop and then addressed the problem of getting her to bed. She was tall, and far from stick-thin. Beneath the shapeless suit she had an old-fashioned quantity of figure which was made for body-hugging dresses and high-cut one-piece bathing suits.

The downside of that was the risk of putting his own back in traction if he wasn't very careful how he lifted her.

But he couldn't leave her slumped in the chair. She'd wake with every muscle screaming in protest.

Or course if she woke up in his arms it wouldn't be just the muscles that screamed.

He shifted his attention to her ear, stroking the tips of his fingers over the warm outer edge in a manner guaranteed to wake all but the soundest of sleepers. No earrings, just tiny gold studs, he noticed. She wore no jewellery of any kind. Wasn't that odd in a woman whose life apparently revolved around the stuff?

All that stirred was a comb, which slipped from its tenuous mooring.

He caught it and stuffed it in his pocket. Then, telling himself he'd undoubtedly be sorry for this later, he bent down and, with one arm beneath her knees and the other round her waist, picked her up.

Her head rolled against his shoulder, combs and pins falling in a noisy shower so that her hair began to fall in loose skeins around her shoulders, catching the light. It was a lot longer than he'd realised.

Why?

Hair was sensuous, almost erotic stuff. Man-bait.

Why would a woman who cared so little about her appearance cling to something that she didn't use to enhance her appearance? Hair that appeared to cause her endless bother?

Why, when on the surface she appeared such a

straightforward, uncomplicated woman, were there so many curious contradictions?

Shifting her dead weight so that he took some of the strain against his chest, he took a cautious step, biting back a harsh expletive as one of his bare feet found the upturned teeth of a comb.

Flora didn't stir. She was dead to the world. Out of it.

As he carried her into her bedroom he began to wish he'd succumbed to temptation and hit the sack himself.

But it didn't last for ever and he finally put her down on the bed as gently as he could. He wasn't sure why he was bothering. She probably wouldn't have woken up if he'd just dropped her on it. And she wouldn't thank him for his trouble anyway.

She'd just look at him with those wary eyes that gave away nothing, absolutely nothing, and tell him he shouldn't have bothered.

What was it with her anyway? He wasn't a monster. Women usually liked him. He had a lot of friends who were women. And a lot of ex-girlfriends who would be happy to see him in hell, he acknowledged. The ones who'd banked on something more permanent.

Maybe Flora was saving time by cutting out the fun bit in between and going straight for the second option.

He'd already decided that she was clever.

He took off her shoes. She had long, narrow feet. Elegant, he thought, although the blue nail polish came as something of a surprise. What kind of woman painted her toenails when no one was going to see them? And didn't paint her fingernails, which they would?

What kind of woman kept long, difficult hair, and then stuffed it up in an untidy bird's nest on top of her head?

One with pretty feet. And a pair of very classy ankles.

He put her shoes beside the bed and set about removing her jacket. It was already creased beyond any remedy other than a very hot iron, which proved the linen was the genuine article. No surprise there. But she'd sleep more comfortably without it, in the jersey silk tank she was wearing beneath it.

He sat on the bed and pulled her up into a sitting position. She slumped against him like an exhausted child, her face squashed against his neck. She'd probably kill him if she woke up now, he thought. But he eased off the jacket and dropped it on the floor and didn't rush to let her go.

If he was going to die, he might as well do something worth dying for. And, with her head still resting against his shoulder, he carefully removed all the pins and combs from her hair.

It descended, heavy and dark, the colour of bittersweet chocolate, over his hands and down her back. He shook it loose, spreading its astonishing silky length through his fingers before he laid her gently back against the pillow and stood back.

Not exactly Sleeping Beauty, but a lot closer than he would ever have imagined when he'd joined her in the back seat of that limousine in the grey chill of a London morning.

It seemed pointless, after such intimacy, to be coy about taking off her trousers. He accomplished that final kindness without difficulty, scarcely pausing to notice that her knickers were not of the plain, functional kind, but were expensive, French, black. And fitted like a second skin.

Or that her legs matched her ankles very nicely.

That would be taking unfair advantage.

He drew the drapes to keep off any curious insects that might fly in, then, closing the louvre doors to the veranda behind him and leaving her to sleep, returned to his delayed breakfast.

To consider the conundrum that was Flora Claibourne. The woman hiding behind the disguise of a plain, spinsterish academic. All she'd left out was a pair of spectacles, he thought.

Ones with heavy tortoiseshell frames—to match the combs.

CHAPTER THREE

FLORA woke feeling muzzy-headed, dry and aching in
all her joints. She also felt slightly hungover, as if
she'd been sitting in one position for too long. Then
she remembered. She had.

Not been drinking too much, just sitting in one position for hours and hours and hours. In a plane. With
Bram Gifford.

Working to avoid talking. Working in an effort to
stave off the tension caused by his presence.

She'd thought she'd got over her problem with men
like him, with their good looks, easy smile, natural
charm. Had it under control.

Apparently not. The moment he'd stepped into the
car it had all come flooding back. The shame. The
painful humiliation.

The hot, sweet rush of desire.

It wasn't fair to blame Bram Gifford, take it out on
him. He was a man who worked hard and played hard.
And made no pretence of being interested in her.
She'd try and be nicer to him. She owed it to India.

She sat up, easing her limbs, then blinked, thinking
there was something wrong with her eyes. But it
wasn't her eyes that were misted, just the sheer drapes
pulled around the bed.

She pushed them aside, swung her feet to the floor
and, finding a bottle of mineral water on the night

table, opened it and took a long drink as she looked about her. She must have crashed fairly spectacularly since she hadn't even noticed the bedroom. It wasn't surprising. She'd been on the go non-stop for the best part of two days.

The only surprise was that she'd managed to get to bed at all. Divested of most of her clothes and with her hair loose, her hairpins and precious antique combs neatly laid out in a row by the bed—all but one of them, anyway—was quite an achievement. She checked her hair for the missing comb, but it must have slipped out somewhere.

The last time she'd flown long-haul she'd woken up with her head on her desk, a crick in her neck that it had taken a week to straighten out and a hairpin jammed in the keyboard of her laptop.

If Bram Gifford had found her like that... Well, she preferred not to think about the kind of impression that would have made. India, quite rightly, would have thrown a hissy fit.

She stood up, did a few stretches. What did the man want, for heaven's sake? He made her so nervous with all that quiet consideration. He was too serious. She didn't believe it. It had to be an act. She just knew he was laughing at her... She stopped herself.

Why would he be laughing? He didn't even want to be here. She had nothing that he wanted.

Except control of Claibourne & Farraday.

As for being serious, wasn't it more likely that he was thoroughly bored? Fed-up with having to trail around after her when he could be hitting the high-life at some fashionable resort packed with pretty girls eager for a holiday flirtation.

At least he hadn't flirted with *her*.

Despite the lack of encouragement, in her experience men like him could rarely resist any opportunity to set female hearts fluttering.

If her mother was busy, they'd practise on her.

Just to keep their hand in.

Most of them had meant no harm. They might even have thought they were being kind. Clearly she'd been desperate for attention.

They had been right. She had. Until she'd learned that not all attention was good. Too late. But she'd learned.

Bram Gifford must wonder what he had to do to get some response from her. She hadn't even squealed entertainingly at the thought of bugs in her sleeping bag. She was no fun at all, she told herself sternly, and caught herself grinning.

And on that cheering note she decided it was time for a shower and something to eat.

Twenty minutes later, wrapped in a towelling robe and with her hair in a turban, she padded back into the bedroom to look for something to wear. She picked up her wristwatch. It was gone three in the afternoon. No wonder she was hungry.

She crossed to the louvre doors and opened them. They were on the east of the island and the veranda was pleasantly shaded—something that Bram Gifford, stretched out on a cane lounger in a pair of shorts and T-shirt, was taking full advantage of.

He had terrific legs, she thought, before she could

stop herself from looking. Sportsman's legs—but more tennis pro than footballer, she thought. She'd become good at spotting the differences. Her mother loved sportsmen.

'Feeling better?' he asked, peeling off a pair of dark glasses and looking up from the latest bestselling legal thriller. Well, he was a lawyer. Maybe he was hoping to pick up some useful tips.

She fought down the urge to beat an immediate retreat to the safety of her bedroom, instead pulling the towel from her hair and shaking it out to dry naturally in the warmth. 'Yes, thanks,' she said, taking a wide-toothed comb from her pocket. Sleeping with her hair lose had its downside, she decided, easing it through the knots. 'Hungry, though.'

'There's an all-day restaurant over by the pool. I checked it out when I had a look around earlier. The food's good. There's a shop, too.' He indicated the book. 'It has all the latest bestsellers. Including yours.'

'They knew I was coming,' she replied, unimpressed. 'You didn't take a nap?'

'I made do with a swim. It's better to tough it out if you can, keep local hours.'

'Yes, well, not all of us are superhuman.' She winced as the comb caught a tangle.

'I'm not criticising, Flora. I got more sleep than you did on the plane, that's all.' He got up. 'Here, let me do that.' He took the comb from her, lifted a hank of wet hair and began to carefully tease through a difficult knot.

She kept very still. He was just combing through her hair, she told herself. It didn't mean a thing. But her body wasn't listening. It hadn't been this close, this intimate with a man in a long time, and every cell seemed to swivel in his direction, attracted by the warm scent of his skin, the small, careful movements of his hand as he worked at the knot. His hair, gleaming in the bright air, slid forward as he bent to his task; the space between his eyes creased in concentration.

He was a walking temptation. Every part of him said, *Touch me*.

'I was working,' she said, and tightened the belt of her robe, as if to keep him out. Then she realised how defensive that looked, how defensive she sounded. She didn't need to be defensive. It wasn't any of his business what she was doing. At least it was, but she had no need to justify herself to him simply because she'd needed to sleep for a while. 'I must have crashed out.'

'With your head on your computer. I thought you'd be more comfortable in bed.' And, having dealt with the knot, he continued to comb through her hair in slow, sensuous sweeps.

She stilled. 'You put me to bed?'

'I tried to wake you,' he assured her. 'But you didn't stir.'

So he'd carried her through to the bedroom, undressed her, drawn the drapes leaving her like something out of a fairy tale? Not Sleeping Beauty, obviously. A less attractive cousin, perhaps.

'Oh.' Well, that certainly explained why the bedroom had looked so unfamiliar when she woke up. She discovered she had to swallow before she managed to say, 'I didn't realise.'

Feeble. Very feeble. She should have just thanked him. Said she'd have done the same for him. Anything would have been better than that pathetic 'oh'. He'd better not smirk, that was all. He'd better just keep looking as serious as he knew how. And she'd better keep looking as if she didn't give a damn.

'Well, thanks,' she added belatedly.

He'd not only undressed her but taken out her hair-pins. He must have held her close, propping her up against that impossibly broad chest, while he'd taken them out one by one. She knew how long it took to find them all. And he'd found every last one.

She felt more exposed by that than if he'd actually stripped her naked. She turned, forcing him to stop combing her hair.

'Your suit looked a bit the worse for wear so I gave it to the housemaid to wash and press,' he said.

'Well, aren't you a regular boy scout?' Which blew any chance of appearing cool in the face of him seeing her in her knickers.

'You must be hungry, Flora,' he said, before she could even begin to think of some graceful way to turn her snappy remark into something suitably grateful.

It didn't help that she didn't want to be grateful. She didn't want to say thank you. She just wished he wasn't standing there with her comb in his hand, evidence of how easily he'd manipulated her into accepting his help. Wished that he was back in London so that she could relax.

'You haven't eaten more than a mouthful since we left London. Get dressed and I'll buy you a late lunch.

You might feel a little less tetchy with something solid inside you.'

About to tell him what to do with his lunch, she felt her common sense finally kick in. He was just trying to be pleasant, which was more than she could say about herself. There was undoubtedly an ulterior motive, but since she knew that she wasn't risking anything by being polite in return, she should probably be making a real effort in that direction. She might even find out something useful for her sister.

'Good move,' she said, with a reasonable stab at a smile. 'When I'm hungry I don't know what I'm saying.'

'Then I'd better make sure it doesn't happen again,' he said, offering her the comb. 'You wouldn't want to say the wrong thing to Dr Myan just because your blood sugar's taken a dip. It would put a major dent in that serious academic image you work so hard to portray. Although why crumpled clothes and a strange hairstyle should equate with brilliance has always been a mystery to me. Maybe you could explain that some time.'

And with that he returned to the sun lounger, put his feet up and, replacing his dark glasses, resumed reading. Leaving her speechless.

Bram peered over the top of his sunglasses, watching her walk away. She was one prickly lady, he thought. And when she smiled he didn't trust her further than he could throw her.

Prickly, complex. Nice ankles, though. Lovely hair—when it was down around her shoulders.

And he'd thought he was going to be bored.

* * *

Flora, on the right side of six hours of solid sleep and a sandwich, felt if not exactly reborn then sufficiently recovered to take an interest in her surroundings.

Flapping away a large iridescent blue insect with her broad-brimmed hat, she looked around her at the poolside restaurant. Only a few of the tables were occupied. One of them by a classically lovely blonde in her late thirties. She was reading, but her gaze had followed Bram as they'd walked across the terrace to a shady spot, lingered for a while. And, although she still had her book open, Flora thought she'd lost interest in the plot. It probably happened wherever Bram Gifford went.

'Where is everybody?' she asked.

'Doing whatever people do around here in the heat of the afternoon,' Bram said without bothering to look around. 'There were more people about earlier when I used the pool,' he said, apparently unaware that he was under close scrutiny.

Maybe it was such an everyday occurrence that he found it easy to ignore. Or maybe he preferred to keep business and pleasure in separate compartments.

Which was fine with her.

'How many?' she asked.

'A couple of dozen, I suppose.'

Or maybe he was just being thoughtful, giving her his undivided attention because he was that kind of man.

How likely was that?

Not likely at all, unless she had something he

wanted. Unless he thought he could use her in his quest to bring down the Claibournes.

'This is a beautiful resort. It seems a shame there are so few people here.'

'It's only been open a few months and it's not exactly on the beaten track,' he pointed out.

'Isn't that what most people are looking for?'

'So they say. But if they found it, it wouldn't be off the beaten track any more, would it?' Then he shrugged. 'Enthuse about the place to the Claibourne & Farraday travel department when you get home if it bothers you. I'm sure the place will be standing room only before you know it.'

An article in one of the Sunday newspapers about the discovery of an unknown princess, dripping in funerary tribute of gold and precious stones, would raise awareness of the island, attract travel writers looking for somewhere undiscovered very nicely too, she thought.

She said, 'I'm not enthusing about anything until I've had a good look round. I'll be taking photographs of the downside of Saraminda as well as the bits the tourist office wants to sell.' Somewhat belatedly she recalled India's advice. 'Maybe you could help with that. How are you on the business end of a camera?'

She wasn't good at dissembling, and to her own ears her casual query sounded horribly false, but that was probably because she *knew* she wasn't being sincere.

'I can handle a point-and-shoot job without cutting off heads or feet,' he confirmed.

That didn't sound particularly convincing either. Bram Gifford looked like a man who'd be totally at home with the most complex equipment. She could very easily imagine his long fingers finessing the lens on a camera—or anything else he considered worth his while. As she watched he laced them together behind his head and leaned back lazily in his chair, so that the soft grey T-shirt he was wearing stretched tight across his chest, riding up to reveal several inches of flat, hard stomach.

'But I'm here to watch—not do your job for you.'

She started. 'What?'

His eyes, behind the dark glasses, were unreadable. There were lines about his mouth that suggested he would be quick to smile, but he wasn't smiling now. The lack of visual clues was unsettling. And deliberate, she suspected. She used the same techniques when she was dealing with jewellery manufacturers. Unfortunately she had never quite managed the trick in her personal life.

'I said—'

But her mind had finally caught up with what he'd said. 'I don't need you to do my job for me,' she said evenly, refusing to rise to such a blatant attempt to annoy her. 'I'm simply concerned that you'll be bored. I was offering you the chance to get involved, that's all. You will have to get involved if you succeed in gaining control of the store.'

Which was rich, coming from her. She did the bare minimum. If she were brutally honest with herself, she'd have to admit that she'd grabbed at Tipi Myan's unexpected offer in an attempt to avoid having Bram Gifford following her about for a month. To avoid having to look as if she knew what a company director was supposed to do, having to justify taking the salary that her father had begun paying her when, still at art college, she'd started designing jewellery for the store.

She'd have been happy to do it for nothing, just to see her designs transformed into precious metal. He'd laughed and said he wanted her under contract before she got poached by someone else.

He wasn't a man to waste his time on his children and it had made her feel special. Wanted. And at the time she'd needed that.

But then she'd become fascinated by the history, the politics behind the precious metals and stones that glittered from the necks and wrists and fingers of the rich and powerful: their attempts to carry their wealth beyond the grave.

The trip to Saraminda had seemed like a gift.

Bad mistake.

In London it would have been a nine-to-five commitment. Bram would have had other calls on his time. Even if he'd taken a break from the office, used vacation time, there would still have been distractions— beautiful distractions, she was sure—to keep him busy. Out here there was no escape from the man.

Remembering how India had looked as she'd begged her to help, she thought that maybe she'd got exactly what she deserved. She had her own totally absorbing, totally satisfying career. How would she feel if someone came along and told her she couldn't do it any more? That she had to give up everything she'd worked to achieve, step back and let someone else take her place? Not because he was more talented, or smarter. But just because he was a man.

Maybe she should invite the blonde to join them, she thought. She would undoubtedly prove a distraction. But that would be feeble…and Bram Gifford would know exactly what she was doing. Instead she looked directly at him.

'Do you really want to get involved, or are the Farradays simply hell-bent on getting their macho way? Just to prove they can? I'm here to work. What about you?'

'But which job is more important?' he returned, ignoring her questions and going straight for the jugular. 'The academic or the commercial one?'

She'd been expecting that from the moment he'd stepped into the car and had her answer ready. But she gave it a minute, as if considering the question. 'I'd say they are symbiotic. They exist in total harmony, each contributing to the other. The store supports my research and travel. The research and travel feeds into my design work.'

'The on-the-spot briefs for the travel department are just an extra, then?' The lazy attitude in the chair was deceptive. His mind was razor-sharp.

She shrugged and didn't attempt to make it sound any more important than it was.

'I can offer a personal impression, a traveller's perspective. I don't pretend to anything more. The travel department finds it useful to have a totally unbiased viewpoint.'

In other words, she had a cup of coffee with the manager of the travel department while he asked how their arrangements for her had worked out.

'Then I guess that answers your question about what

you're going to do until the museum vaults open after the holiday.'

She didn't ask. She waited for him to tell her, since he was going to anyway.

'You'll be playing tourist.'

'There's only one site I'm interested in at the moment.'

'You heard Dr Myan. It's off limits.' There was a warning note in his voice. 'Dangerous. I'm sure there are other places worth a visit.'

'What's the matter, Bram? Put off by his talk of a long walk? Uphill?'

'I didn't bring my walking boots,' he reminded her.

'No.' But *she* wasn't about to give up. She was going to look at that tomb whatever it took. Since Bram Gifford wasn't volunteering to help her—and why should he when his only interest was Claibourne & Farraday business?—she let it go with a shrug. 'Well, I'm sure you're right. There'll be plenty to see.'

'Why don't you start this evening? Take a taxi into Minda, soak up a little of the local atmosphere. Try out a restaurant, perhaps.'

She noted the 'you'. Was he finally getting the message that he was free to amuse himself?

'Don't you want to come along and take notes?' she asked.

'I've seen you eat. You do it very well. Mouth neatly closed, good technique with the fork. But I don't think I'd buy tickets.'

She deserved that. She *had* told him he could follow her or not, as he pleased. More than once. It would be churlish to be cross now if he chose to take the hint, although she didn't much relish the thought of wandering around a strange city after dark by herself. But she wasn't about to admit it. Instead she shrugged and said, 'Fair enough.'

She gave her full attention to the distant seascape. A freighter leaving the island. A couple of fishing boats out in the bay. Then her gaze strayed to the blonde and it occurred to her that she might have met Bram earlier, that he might already have arranged a more interesting diversion.

'Will you eat here?' she asked.

'I shouldn't think so. There's not much in the way of atmosphere.'

'No? Well, if you want to share a taxi into town, just say the word. I'm sure there's more than one restaurant.'

'Bound to be.'

'I'm sure you'll find all the…um…atmosphere you want there.' And this time she looked directly at the other woman. Behind dark glasses, it was difficult to judge where Bram's gaze was directed.

'That's true. Of course since you will be on Claibourne & Farraday business—'

'I always try to combine a little business with pleasure,' she agreed.

'—maybe I *should* come along.'

He'd been winding her up? 'Don't worry about it, Mr Gifford. I'll make notes. You can look at them when you have a spare moment. You just go and find some congenial—'

'Bram,' he said, before she could tell him what he

should find. Then, to make his point, added, 'We're colleagues after all. Flora.'

'Don't worry about it, Bram,' she finally conceded, ignoring his slight stress on the word 'colleagues'. The 'Mr Gifford' had been her own little wind-up, after all. 'Find a bar, some congenial company,' she added, turning the key a little tighter. 'Do whatever you'd usually do.' She paused. 'Just enjoy yourself.'

'I think maybe I should tag along with you, instead.'

Flora turned to look at him. There was winding up and there was just plain damn rude.

'After all, when the Farradays regain control of C&F at the end of June,' he continued—and the smile that went with this remark was not calculated to take the sting out of his words, 'I'll be the one briefing the travel department.'

Flora, about to remind him that this wasn't by any means a foregone conclusion, and he shouldn't stress himself, was struck by a thought of such brilliance that she discovered she didn't have to pretend to smile any more. She was doing it for real.

'Well, if you insist.' She shrugged, as if she didn't care one way or the other. 'But tomorrow I'd better get in some serious sightseeing—' she flapped again at a persistent insect '—since I won't be able to do anything else. I'll hire a car or something.'

'Or something?'

'Maybe a Jeep would be better.' His expression suggested something air-conditioned would be a lot more comfortable. 'Something fairly rugged, anyway. The roads might be a bit...' she faltered under his unwavering gaze, which was made all the more unnerving by the dark lenses that shadowed his expression. 'A bit, um, rough.'

'They seemed perfectly adequate on the way from the airport,' he said. 'Or did you have somewhere particular in mind for this exploring? Somewhere off-road, perhaps?'

She laughed a little self-consciously. 'How could I? I don't know anything about the place. There must be interesting historic sights, though.'

'There always seem to be,' he said, without much enthusiasm.

'And they won't all be placed conveniently next to a good road. Did you notice if the shop has map of the island?' She dropped her napkin by her plate and stood up, not liking the speculative twitch of his brows. 'Why don't you order some coffee while I go and have a look? Unless you really intend to follow me everywhere,' she added quickly. 'Though I'm not sure what you could learn from watching me shop.'

He slid the dark glasses down his long, straight nose and for a moment considered her washed-out khaki shirtdress. It owed nothing to style and everything to utility, and was remarkable, she knew, only for the size and quantity of its pockets. It was why she'd chosen it.

'Nothing very useful,' he said, after an epic pause.

She didn't actually smile; it wasn't a remark that warranted pleasure. But it pleased her, nonetheless. She didn't dress to lure the opposite sex, but for her own comfort and convenience. She'd tried it the other way and it had caused her nothing but pain.

Instead, she scooped up her now dry hair, twisted it

into a knot and, jamming on her hat in order to keep it in place, went in search of a map. A treasure map. And with a bit of luck someone who could mark the spot with an X...

CHAPTER FOUR

BRAM signalled a waiter, ordering coffee without taking his eyes off Flora as she made her way around the pool to the resort shop. She moved with a fluidity and grace that belied the prickly exterior, the terrible clothes.

He just knew that she would look a lot more appealing out of her clothes than in them.

She was, he decided, a woman of hidden depths. She'd never be beautiful; her features were too bold for that. But she wasn't as plain as first impressions would suggest either. The image she projected was just a front, a disguise. Why did she feel the need to hide?

He already had a pretty good idea why she didn't want him with her while she bought a map, listening while she made enquiries about 'interesting historic sites'.

She'd have to be a lot more careful if she wanted to keep secrets from him. A map, a Jeep and a 'eureka' smile—a smile that had lit up her face in a way that exposed anything that had gone before as a total sham—could only mean one thing.

She had a free day on her hands, a day with nothing to do but twiddle her thumbs, and it didn't take a genius to work out that thumb-twiddling didn't come naturally to Flora Claibourne. Or that she wouldn't be sidetracked by the suggestion of danger. She wanted a look at this mysterious tomb and if Dr Myan wouldn't take her there then she was quite prepared to make enquiries, seek it out and go there on her own.

Correction: not on her own. She wasn't that stupid. She wasn't stupid at all. No wonder she'd smiled. She was going to use his promise—his threat—to stay with her every minute of this trip. Use him. His presence was the one thing that made an unauthorised visit to the mountains possible. Which meant it was up to him to make sure she didn't get there.

He might be wrong, but, for all his smiles, he didn't think the Minister of Antiquities would be exactly thrilled to discover that his tame academic had gone exploring by herself. Why that should be was not his concern. His only problem was keeping her from harm's way. It shouldn't be difficult. Unless, of course, she turned out to be the one woman he'd ever met who could read a map. Or understand the basics of the internal combustion engine.

How likely was that?

The blonde sitting a few tables away finally managed to catch his eye. He had the impression she wanted to talk. She had no chance. He liked the company of women—most women—with one unshakable exception. He avoided lonely women of a certain age, a certain style, staking out holiday resorts.

Just to make the point that he was fully occupied, he turned a full-blown smile on Flora as she rejoined him. 'Did you find what you were looking for?'

Startled by the warmth of his welcome, she fumbled her bag as she dropped it on the table, spilling out a tourist map and a guidebook.

'What's this?' He picked up a flat, perspex compass. 'What kind of sightseeing requires the use of a compass?' he asked, looking up, inviting her to confide in him.

She didn't. What she did was take it from him and put it in one of her copious pockets. 'I never travel without a compass.'

'And you had the nerve to call me a boy scout?' Then, 'Why didn't you buy a proper map of the island to go with it?'

'Isn't this a proper map?' she asked, all innocence, as she opened up the simple tourist map that showed main roads and routes to tourist sites, with the mountains no more than a series of cartoon-style peaks.

'It'll do,' he admitted. 'Just so long as your idea of sightseeing doesn't include a trek through the jungle in search of this "lost princess" of yours.'

'The princess has been found. It's the tomb that's missing.'

'Not missing. Just off-limits,' he reminded her.

'You don't think I should try to find it?'

'What part of "off-limits" didn't you understand?'

'I understand the words. It's the reason that baffles me.'

'You heard Tipi Myan. It's unsafe.'

'So it's a bit shaky—but I'm not stupid. I wouldn't go scrambling over something that's about to fall on me. I just want to see it for myself.'

'Forget it, Flora.' He waited for some reassurance that she would do just that. When it didn't come he said, 'Please tell me that you know I'm right.'

She adopted a pose, her hand lightly touching her

breast in a manner that implied faint astonishment. Then, with the *faux* mockery of a flirtatious woman of certain type, said, 'But you're a man, Bram. How could you be anything other than right?'

He knew it was just a distraction to avoid giving him the assurance he sought. Beneath the mockery, though, he caught a glimpse of that other Flora Claibourne—the hidden woman, the touch of steel obscured by her tedious hair and clothes. And he was more distracted than he would have believed possible.

'A simple affirmation will do.'

'"Yes" is the word every man wants to hear,' she replied, dropping the act as quickly as she'd adopted it. 'But, if it makes you happy, I'll promise you I wouldn't dream of trekking through the jungle. How would I know where to start?'

How indeed? Was it the sun or a guilty blush that had turned her cheekbones a faint pink?

He didn't press it, though. Instead he picked up the guidebook and flipped through it. 'I don't see any mention of your treasure or the tomb.' There were just the usual tourist traps: ornate pagodas, dancers, craft centres.

'No? Well, it's too recent, I suppose.'

'Have you any clue to its location?' he asked. Abandoning the guidebook and pushing back the coffee cups, he laid out the very basic tourist map she'd bought. 'Didn't Dr Myan tell you anything?' She'd need some idea where to start if she wasn't hoping to 'stumble across it'.

'You heard him. A long walk. Uphill.'

But she'd discovered something, he could see.

Beneath that dreary dress she was fizzing like a hang-
over cure on New Year's Day. It seemed that Flora
Claibourne couldn't keep a secret to save her life,
which was promising. He wondered how much she
knew about India Claibourne's plans to repel their
claim on C&F. And what it would take to loosen her
up, crack the façade.

'It's a valuable heritage site,' she continued. 'I
imagine they want to protect it from treasure-hunters.
They could do a lot of damage if they hoped to find
more gold.'

'If the ruins don't damage them first,' he countered.
'By falling on them.'

'That, too.'

'I'm sure it's well guarded.'

'Why? The gold is locked up in the museum.
Remoteness and secrecy are its best protection.'

'When two people know something, it's no longer
a secret.'

'No? Well, anyway,' she said, changing the subject,
'I've organised the rental of a four-wheel drive for the
whole of our stay here.'

'A Jeep?'

'Don't look like that,' she protested. 'It's not army
surplus. It's brand-new, built for the luxury end of the
market and fully air-conditioned. If you want to drive
it yourself you'll have to give details of your licence
at the desk.' She glanced at him. 'But maybe you'd
rather arrange your own personal transport?'

'Why would I do that?'

'So that you can do your own thing.'

And she could do hers? Had he underestimated her? Would she really go off on her own?

'I may be wrong, but I don't get the impression that visiting the local tourist traps is high on your list of things to do on holiday.'

She would.

Terrific.

'Why do you persist in this illusion that while you're working I'm on holiday?'

'It's okay. Really. I won't tell if you'd rather spend tomorrow by the pool...recovering from jet lag.' Her glance flickered towards the blonde.

'You've got me all wrong,' he said, abandoning any idea of a relaxing day at the beach. She was wrong if she thought he could be diverted by a poolside romance. But not that wrong. He avoided manufactured tourist sights like the plague, but the small still voice of lawyer's intuition warned him not to let her out of his sight. They were a long way from home in a place where tourists were something of a novelty and, whatever either them of thought of the situation, they were still partners. 'I love sightseeing,' he assured her. 'Let's make a day of it.'

Flora shrugged. Bram Gifford, the lawyer, was lying through his teeth. He didn't want to play tourist any more than she did, but was apparently determined to keep her from playing 'hunt the tomb'. No problem.

She was happy to indulge him by making plans to spend the following day sightseeing with him, if that was what made him happy.

'Okay. What about the primate orphanage?' She showed him a picture of an appealing infant monkey in the guidebook. 'They rear orphans and then, when they're old enough, move them up here—'

'To the mountains?'

'Where they can live in a semi-protected environment.'

'That's very admirable, but I thought you'd be eager to get a taste of the local culture.' Taking the guidebook from her, Bram countered with a picturesque palace. It was on an island, by a lake, in a valley. 'I'd have said this was more your cup of tea. All that gilding. And the Royal Botanical Gardens are not to be missed.'

'Really? How do you know?'

'It says so. Right here,' he said, pointing to a 'Not to be Missed' flash over the picture. Flora leaned closer to get a better look and her shoulder brushed against his. She moved back slightly, but not before he caught a trace of her scent. Warm and spicy. And very faint. As if she was declaring that she was a woman, but doing it very, very quietly.

Like keeping her long hair, but putting it up in those hideous combs. Painting her toenails blue. Wearing sexy knickers. A private statement of her femininity.

'I wonder if they've considered the tourist potential of weddings?' he went on. 'I was best man at a wedding in the botanical gardens in Singapore last year. It's a big tourist market,' he reminded her.

'In that case we must certainly visit the botanical gardens. And this weaving centre, too. I want to look at the local cloth. And there are temple dancers...' Then, almost as an afterthought, 'It might be best if we started at the primate centre, since that's the furthest from here. Then we can work our way back, ticking off the attractions as we go.'

'You think so? It's a bit predictable, don't you think? You've seen one monkey, you've seen them all. My vote—as a potential tourist—goes to the palace,' he said.

'Excuse me, but I'm not running a democracy here. You don't have a vote. We start at the monkey sanctuary. And, since it's going to be a long day, I think we should ask the hotel to put us up a packed lunch. There's a beach starred here,' she said. 'It'll make a great place to stop for a swim and a picnic.'

'Really? How do they feel about skinny-dipping in this part of the world?'

'What?'

'You didn't bring a swimsuit,' he reminded her.

'Oh, no. Well, there's a boutique in the hotel; I saw it just now when I bought the map,' she said, quickly, with a reprise of the blush. 'I could buy one from there.'

'So you could.'

'You don't sound exactly eager.'

'Was I supposed to be eager? I'm sorry. Let me try that again. You could buy a swimsuit from the boutique. Or maybe a bikini,' he added. The eagerness with which he said this wasn't entirely fake.

There was something about the secretiveness of her sexuality that awakened his interest. Something about the thought of stripping away her body armour that seemed to bring out the caveman instinct in him. His fingers itched to pluck that hat from her head and watch her hair tumble around her shoulders, down her back. To peel away the layers one by one until he'd got to the heart of the woman. Found the true Flora Claibourne.

'I meant eager for a picnic on the beach,' she said, with assumed boredom.

'Oh, right. Cancel the eagerness. In my experience sand and food aren't a great combination.'

'All right, forget the beach. We'll lunch *al fresco* amongst the wild orchids at the botanical gardens,' she suggested, 'and consider its viability as a wedding venue.' She leaned over and, careful not to touch him, turned the pages of the guidebook until she found it. 'It says here that there are butterflies the size of tea-plates—'

'I'll bet it doesn't say anything about ants the size of rats. The kind that bite.'

'You've got a real problem with insects, haven't you, Bram?' She turned to him, her forehead creased in a slightly puzzled expression that didn't fool him for a minute. 'Have you considered therapy?'

The only problem he had was with a woman—and it wasn't the kind that therapy could fix. 'Thanks for your concern, but I'll stick with the repellent.' He wondered, briefly, if he used enough, whether it might repel her.

'Lucky you. I'm allergic to it.'

That would do it, too. Except that he'd made up his mind to stick close and make sure she didn't get into trouble. Which was not only a nuisance, but was also something of a surprise. She didn't look like a woman who went looking for trouble. Quite the reverse, in fact. She looked like a woman determined to avoid it at all costs. Or maybe she just avoided the kind that came packaged with testosterone.

Remembering Jordan's suggestion that he might 'even the score', he thought she was right to be cautious. The trick would be not to alert her…to make a friend of her first…

He made a conscious effort to stop right there, before his mind started getting inventive.

And yet, and yet… There was something hidden, undiscovered about this woman, and that was his brief. To find out what made Flora Claibourne tick. Discover any little weakness. Uncover secrets.

He decided to start with the simple things. 'Is there anything else I should know about you?' he asked. 'In the event of a medical emergency?'

'Like what?'

Like a pile of ruins falling on her. 'I don't know. That's why I'm asking,' he said, with a touch of exasperation. This woman could turn the simplest question into an interrogation. 'Do you have a rare blood group? Are you allergic to penicillin? Nuts?' Why was he even asking?

'No. Just insect repellent. I use essential oils instead. Did you know that we have a qualified aromatherapist in the store now? She made up a special blend for me when I went to Africa last year.'

'Does it work?'

'I have no way of comparing results,' she replied. 'But it smells a lot nicer than the chemical stuff.' She offered her wrist for his opinion.

If any other woman had made that gesture he'd have known exactly what she wanted and he'd have cradled the wrist in his hand, lifted it closer, kissed the pale skin…after which just about anything would have been possible. Flora Claibourne was a complete mystery to him, however, and he did none of those things, but instead got to his feet.

'Good grief,' she said, 'it's supposed to repel insects, not men.'

'Relax.' He glanced at his watch. 'If we're going out this evening I'd better catch a couple of hours' sleep if I don't want to end up face-down in the soup. If I haven't emerged by seven-thirty, will you give me a knock?'

'Sleep?'

She made irony into an art form, he thought. But compared with yesterday's silence it was an advance. Of sorts.

'Isn't that a little feeble? I thought you were a man of iron, determined to keep local hours.'

'In a hot climate, local hours usually involve a siesta. Especially when you're on holiday.'

She put her hand up to hold onto her wide-brimmed hat as she tipped her head back to look up at him. 'But you're not on holiday,' she reminded him. 'At least that's what you keep telling me.'

And he meant it. If he were on holiday he wouldn't be with this tiresome female. Suddenly irritable, he said, 'Your nose is going pink. I'd advise using zinc sunblock. Do you have some?'

By way of reply, she opened her shoulder bag and took out a small pot of cream. She opened it and dipped her finger in before stroking a thick white band of it down the centre of her nose.

'Happy?' she asked.

'Ecstatic,' he replied.

Flora's eyes lingered on the long, powerful legs carrying Bram away towards the lobby of the resort complex. Purposeful, powerful and leading the gaze inevitably upward to a backside built to undermine the will of even the strongest-minded woman.

It didn't seem right that one man should have so much. Fortunately he didn't have everything. Girls had no doubt been falling over themselves to make his day since he was old enough to notice them. It wasn't reasonable to expect that he should also be gracious, warm-hearted and agreeable. Why would he be, when he didn't have to bother? Human nature just wasn't like that.

Bram Gifford didn't want to be with her because she didn't live up to his elevated standards of superficial attractiveness. She'd read the file India had compiled on the man. He was a man of two halves. The daytime part was a successful, hardworking corporate lawyer. After dark he turned into a playboy with a penchant for lovely women. In the plural. He didn't believe in long-term relationships.

Her reason for not wanting to be with him was more complicated. He was, if anything, too close to her own particular fantasy package. If he'd been nice, she'd have had to work a lot harder to dislike him.

As it was, she told herself, she should be grateful that it took so little effort.

She sat for a while, taking her time about drinking her coffee, wanting to be sure that he wasn't going to come back, watching the lonesome blonde. She was exactly the kind of woman Bram Gifford was usually seen with. A little older, perhaps, but he was on holiday. He could afford to let his standards slip a little and she'd make the perfect distraction.

But he seemed oblivious to her charms, and Flora hated the little give-away lift to her spirits at the thought. Angry with herself for giving a damn, she reached into the depths of her shoulder bag and retrieved the other, more detailed map she'd bought and pushed carefully to the bottom of her bag.

The one that hadn't fallen out.

The one which the assistant in the shop had so helpfully marked with the site of the tomb.

And, while Bram Gifford took his belated siesta, she stayed by the pool and worked out exactly what she was going to do the next day. Once she'd lost her shadow.

She should feel bad about deceiving him, she knew. But demonstrating the resourcefulness of the Claibourne women was all part of her brief.

The sun was setting fast when she finally made a move to return to the cottage, take a shower and change for her dinner date with Bram.

The lovely blonde still hadn't moved and Flora felt a sudden qualm of unease, a feeling that she should speak to her, ask her if everything was all right. But as she made a move towards her the receptionist crossed the terrace with a message for the woman and Flora, after a moment's hesitation, let it go.

CHAPTER FIVE

FLORA preferred to travel light, and she'd seen no reason to change the habit of a lifetime for her trip to Saraminda just because Bram Gifford was along for the trip.

Back in London, where her head ruled, it had seemed a very good reason to stick to her routine.

She had a black go-anywhere two-piece consisting of a long tunic top and a pair of loose trousers that covered most occasions. It could be packed without fuss, washed without requiring the services of an iron and, since it had never been at the cutting edge of fashion, it never dated.

She shook it out, hung it over a door and regarded it with new eyes, wondering how he'd see it. Wondering if it was time to retire it, trade it in for something new. Wishing that she'd got something lively and exciting to wear for their evening in Minda. Something that would wipe that *look* off his face.

The kind of wishing, in other words, that could only end in tears. Her tears. She'd done that, made a total fool of herself, and made that 'never again' promise to herself that all girls made in those circumstances. In her case she'd meant it, and stuck to it. It hadn't been particularly difficult. Once you'd seen through the act, really seen through it for the selfish sham it

72

72

was, it would be an act of wilful stupidity to be taken in again.

She'd thought she was clever. No make-up. No sexy hairstyle or clothes. Definitely no glamorous earrings.

Maybe the truth of the matter was that she just hadn't had sufficient temptation.

She twisted her hair a little tighter than usual, adding a few extra pins to make up for the missing comb. She wasn't going to ask Bram Gifford if he'd seen it. He'd seen altogether too much when he'd relieved her of them.

Why on earth had he gone to so much trouble when all he'd had to do was drop her on the bed and walk away? Okay, so taking off her shoes made good sense, but as for the rest—had he been kind or merely curious?

As she pushed her feet into a pair of low-heeled sandals she noticed the blue polish on her toenails and got her answer. Curious. She wiggled her toes and grinned. He must have been disappointed after that promising start. What, she wondered, had he made of them when he removed her shoes?

She'd bet he had an opinion.

And she'd just bet it wasn't complimentary, she thought, picking up her bag and the keys to the car and walking out onto the veranda to wait for her date. She hadn't had to give Bram a wake-up call. The sound of his shower had been ample evidence that he was awake.

He was already waiting for her, leaning against the low rail, staring out at the starlit ocean. He'd gone for casual, too. A coloured collarless shirt, open at the neck, the cuffs folded back to reveal strong wrists. Cream cotton trousers. Hair slithering attractively over his forehead. The difference was, he looked good enough to eat.

He half turned, without straightening, and looked at her for a moment, his eyes expressionless. It was a look she was getting to know very well. It said, wow—all lower case. No capital letters or exclamation marks. And, What have I done to deserve an evening in the company of this woman? A groan, rather than exclamation of joy at his good fortune.

Totally underwhelmed, in fact. Exactly the effect she'd aimed for. She should have been happier at hitting the mark so perfectly. She reached up to tuck in a comb that was already beginning to work its way free.

'I haven't kept you waiting?' she asked. 'You did say eight o'clock?'

'I'm in no hurry,' he said. That was probably the understatement of the year. He couldn't have been in less of a hurry if he'd been asleep. But he straightened and held out his hand for the keys to the off-roader.

She ignored it, stepped down onto the path and, despite the heat, headed briskly in the direction of the car park, leaving him to follow or not, as he wished. Okay, she'd dressed for underwhelming and she'd got the response she'd aimed for, but politeness cost nothing.

Or had he already worked out that, playing by her rules, there was no way he could win? If he'd offered some formal, meaningless compliment, she would have been mentally berating him for insincerity right now.

She found herself smiling a little. She'd never doubted that he was clever, but maybe she'd had a little trouble seeing past the playboy image. Bram caught up with her and put himself between her and the Jeep door.

'I'll drive, Flora,' he said.

Not *that* clever, then. He was just an average old-fashioned chauvinist male who couldn't handle being driven by a woman. It was scarcely any wonder that he didn't think her capable of sitting on the board of a multimillion-pound business.

Okay, so she didn't particularly want that honour, but it should be her choice, not his. Never had she felt more determined to assert her right to that choice. Or to the driver's seat.

'You want to drive, Bram, you hire your own transport,' she said, her smile deepening.

'I've been to the desk and cleared the insurance, if you're concerned,' he said.

'I'm not in the slightest bit concerned, and when you're on your own you can drive with my blessing,' she said, and, keys in hand, waited for him to move aside. He didn't.

'No offence, Flora, but you can't control your hair. I'm not prepared to find out the hard way if that applies to everything else in your life. When you're on your own *you* can do what you like, but when I'm on board I'm driving.'

Without breaking eye contact, he reached for her wrist, lifted her hand and helped himself to the keys.

It was over before the urgent flash from her brain to tighten her grip reached her fingers.

'Thank you.' He opened the driver's door, then, when she didn't move, said, 'I'd open the door for you, but you modern women are so touchy about things like that.'

'You…' She caught at her breath, stopping the angry words before they left her mouth. She doubted that he was deliberately going out of his way to make her angry. He really wasn't that interested. Losing control would hurt no one but herself.

'Yes?' he prompted.

'You may be right about my hair,' she admitted, tucking a comb a little more firmly in place. 'As for my driving—well, I have nothing to prove. But if being driven by a woman threatens your masculinity, then, please, be my guest.'

She walked away, round the front of the vehicle, and climbed into the passenger seat. She didn't need a man to help her into a vehicle of any kind. In fact she could handle anything that came her way without the assistance of a Y chromosome.

And sometimes walking away was all it took to make you a winner.

She glanced across at Bram. He was standing just where she'd left him, a puzzled frown creasing the space between his honey-coloured eyes, as if trying to work out how, by letting him get away with it, she'd effectively turned the tables on him.

Which suggested that it had been deliberate after all—Bram Gifford had been going out of his way to make her lose her temper, her self-control.

Well, tough. She didn't do that. Not any more. Which didn't mean she wouldn't exact retribution. Tomorrow, she promised herself. You'll pay for that tomorrow when you discover that you'll be taking the sightseeing tour on your own.

For now, though, she just smiled and said, 'I don't suppose you've found one of my combs anywhere? I seem to have lost one.'

He tossed the keys up a few inches, snatched them from the air and then climbed aboard. 'Maybe you should do yourself a favour and get a haircut,' he said, as he fitted them into the ignition.

'I nearly did that once.' Personal remarks were off-limits in a business relationship, but she was happy to play along. There was nothing he could say on that subject that could hurt her. She had scar tissue inches thick.

He started the engine and headed for the road. 'What stopped you?' he asked, looking both ways before pulling out in the traffic. Not at her. 'Cutting your hair?'

'Not a what. A who. His name was Sam. Or maybe it was Seb...' She pretended to think about it, then shook her head. 'Something beginning with S.'

'A man?'

Of course it was a man. A man who'd run his fingers through her hair, brushed it until it shone and told her that it was pure silk, that it was her most beautiful feature. That she should never have it cut.

Of course she'd never let him see it tangled, or wet. Only sleek, glossy perfection.

Every day, as she brushed it out, she remembered his words.

Every day as she pinned it up she reminded herself never to believe such lies ever again.

'Close your mouth, Bram. That much surprise isn't polite.'

Bram's mouth hadn't been open, but it might as well have been, and he knew he deserved the metaphorical slap. He was being unutterably boorish. 'My surprise was a perfectly natural reaction to the suggestion that one of the Claibourne women would ever consider doing something a man suggested,' he said. He just couldn't seem to stop himself.

'My only defence is that I was very young at the time.'

How young? Sixteen, seventeen? What had she looked like then? Innocent? Her dreams still intact? He pushed the thought away. 'That would explain it,' he said.

It didn't explain his behaviour, though, beyond the fact that he'd assumed she'd make an effort with her appearance since they were going out for dinner. Just as he'd been planning to make an effort to be nice—see if he could make her laugh sufficiently to relax a little and forget her damned hair for an hour. Maybe his motives weren't entirely altruistic, but it didn't matter a damn anyway. She wasn't prepared to meet him halfway.

She'd appeared wearing a dreary black two-piece and low-heeled sandals. She hadn't even bothered with a touch of lipstick. How much trouble would that have been?

Nowhere near as much trouble as painting her toe-nails blue.

Who had merited that much effort? The boyfriend whose name she pretended not to remember?

Why did he care?

Maybe, he admitted as he drove in silence towards town, it was because he wasn't used to coming in second. A very long way second.

He'd assumed that all he'd have to do was smile and Miss Flora Claibourne would open up and tell him all her little secrets. Maybe he'd had it too easy for too long. He'd become complacent, needed a challenge to sharpen him up.

He glanced across at her. She returned his look with a textbook smile. The kind an actress might practise in the mirror. He frowned as he gave his full attention to the road, avoiding milling pedestrians who seemed to have no traffic sense, tense and irritable.

'Why don't we park somewhere and join the crowds?' Flora suggested when they'd reached the centre of Minda and been reduced to crawling along at snail's pace by the crowds flocking through the streets in a holiday mood. 'Could you squeeze into that space over there, do you think?' Then, 'It's a bit tight. I'd never attempt it myself, of course, but men are so much better at parallel parking.'

And Bram discovered that it was Flora who had made him laugh, not the other way around.

'Did I say something funny?' she asked.

'You really must get a pair of false eyelashes to go with that delicate little flower act,' he said, as he reversed neatly into the space she'd indicated. 'Really long ones, that you can flutter.' He switched off the engine and turned to her. 'I'm sorry, okay? It's not personal. It's not even a ''women drivers'' thing. I hate being driven by anyone.' He took the keys from the ignition. 'I guess I need to be in control.'

'You're not a bit sorry, Bram. You're just a dinosaur. You and your cousins are in a class all by yourselves. Farradaysaurus. So far behind the times that you're practically extinct. You're just refusing to lie down and die.'

'Stubborn, too, you think?' He turned to her with a smile. 'It appears that I need help. Maybe you'd better—'

'No.' She held up a hand to stop him. 'Let me guess. This is where you become an instantly reformed character and gracefully offer me the keys so that I can drive back to the hotel, right? And I'm supposed to be grateful for the opportunity to drink nothing but soda all night while you get mellow on the local booze?'

It wasn't what he'd had in mind, but he didn't blame her for thinking it. And she deserved to think she'd won a round. 'You've got me. Come on, let's find somewhere to eat and you can list all my faults.'

'It may take a while.'

'I don't doubt it. I'll listen attentively if you'll put me out of my misery and tell me why you've painted your toenails blue.'

She glanced down at her toes and wiggled them. 'Is it the painting or the colour that interests you?'

'You decide.' He caught her hand as they joined the mill of people, tightening his grip as she made an instinctive movement to pull away. 'It would be easy to lose you in this crowd.'

'There you go again, you see. I'm not a child, Bram. I'm twenty-six years old and a director of the finest department store in London. What I'm not is helpless.'

'Indulge me,' he said. 'I'm a dinosaur, remember?'

Flora distrusted him even more when he was being nice, when he was trying to make her laugh. But she shrugged and, leaving her hand clasped protectively in his, momentarily closed her eyes and reminded herself that she was in control here. Of herself. Of the situation. Nothing he could do or say would fool her for a minute.

'Flora?'

She opened her eyes to find that he was looking at her, a slight frown creasing the space between his eyes. 'Sorry,' she said. 'I was just trying to decide which kind.' She smiled. 'One of the big, slow ones, the kind with a very small brain a long way from anything important. Or one of those terrible flesh-tearing creatures—'

'I get the picture, but do me a favour and keep the outcome of your deliberations to yourself. Whatever you decide it's not going to be flattering, and I'd really rather not hear it.'

'Oh, *please*!' she said, dismissing this out of hand. 'If my mother taught me anything it's that there is nothing the male of the species enjoys more than hearing about himself.'

'She would surely know. Go through that many husbands and you're bound to pick up some useful information. Along with the seven-figure financial settlements.'

'She doesn't do that any more.'

'No, of course not. This time she decided to vary the plot and marry for pure lust.'

He'd checked up on her? Her background? Why was she surprised? She didn't let the smile slip by so much as micron. 'At least she knows what she wants. And gets it every time,' she added, as if he'd proved her case for her. 'That's how I know you're absolutely panting to hear that you've been classified a close cousin to the Tyrannosaurus Rex.'

'I think ''panting'' overstates the case.' And he smiled right back at her. 'Breathing a little heavily is all I'm prepared to admit to.'

'Don't worry, when I make my mind up you'll be the first person I tell.' And she turned away from a gaze that was suddenly sharper, more intense. 'Are you desperately hungry?' she asked, looking about her at the busy shops, restaurants, market stalls. Anything to divert her mind from the unexpected intimacy, the edgy danger of close contact with a man she had every reason to believe planned to take advantage of the slightest sign of weakness. To divert herself from the warm contact of his palm against hers, the light pressure of his thumb against the back of her fingers. It was a personal challenge. Pulling away would be an admission of defeat. Admitting that it affected her. 'I'd really like to take a look at these stalls.'

'Lead the way. This is your show,' he said.

'I'd like to think you believe that, but I'm not convinced.'

'You've got me here, haven't you?'

So she had. And she wasn't entirely sure why he'd decided to spend the evening with her rather than pick up the open invitation from the lonely blonde beside the pool. But as she began to walk down the street, stopping to look at anything that caught her eye, she was under no illusion; his presence was for his benefit rather than hers.

Then she let it go and began to concentrate on the activity around them. There were street vendors selling all kinds of freshly cooked food, the spicy scent of meat and vegetables mingling enticingly with pastries.

There were stalls piled with weird masks, small stone gods, wood carvings, and her busy brain logged them away against an opportunity to use them.

Bram went further and bought a terrifying spirit mask for a friend's child, holding it up for her to get the effect.

'His mother will love you when he has nightmares,' Flora said, turning to a display of locally produced jewellery to check it out.

'He'll be the envy of all his friends.' Bram picked up a pair of long silver earrings from amongst those she was looking at and held them up to her ear. They brushed against her neck. 'Why don't you wear jewellery?' he asked. 'Shouldn't you fly the flag for your own designs?'

'India and Romana do a far better job than I can in that department,' she said, shivering at the cool touch of the metal, the warmth of his hand against her neck. She took them from him to take a closer look. They were handmade, a pictogram—some word from the

Saramindan language. And what they lacked in finish they more than made up for in dash.

She picked out half a dozen pairs, then turned to the stall-holder and engaged in some good-humoured haggling, complicated by the fact that he spoke no English. They did pretty well, with fingers and pointing and US dollars by way of universal currency. 'Have you noticed that there's no gold?' she asked, while her purchases were wrapped.

'You wouldn't expect to find gold jewellery on sale at a street market, would you?'

'Perhaps not.' She put her purchases in her bag and let it go. 'It doesn't matter.'

'You're wondering where the gold came from for your princess? There's none on the island?'

'Not that I'm aware of. There might have been a small deposit, long played out. Or maybe it was brought here. Traded for some other precious resource.'

'Maybe the early Saramindans were pirates,' Bram volunteered. 'And they just stole it.'

'That's a possibility. Or maybe she didn't live here at all. Maybe she was taken sick on some voyage and her people stopped here and buried her with all the ceremony she was due.'

'To the extent that they'd stay here long enough to build a special tomb?'

'If she was important enough. If she was a precious daughter, or wife or mother. It's the history that makes it interesting, don't you think?'

'That's why it's important for you to actually see the ruins?'

'Absolutely. Without some atmosphere anything I write is just a glorified inventory. Interesting, but lacking in romance or mystery.' Then, realising she was getting a bit carried away and because she didn't want to make too big a thing of it, she said, 'I don't suppose it really matters. Oh, just look at that!'

She moved quickly on to a stall piled with local cloth—some woven with silver thread, some richly patterned with animals and geometric shapes. She draped a piece of cloth over her shoulder, turning to him. 'What do you think?'

'I think you'd probably do better adding the weaving centre to tomorrow's sight seeing tour,' Bram said. 'And you'd have proper lighting to see the colours.'

She'd completely forgotten the sightseeing itinerary for the following day. But then, it had been a mere distraction, to reassure him that she wouldn't ever think of doing something stupid like going to take a look at the tomb by herself. 'If this is the quality of cloth available I'll go to the weaving centre first thing on Sunday morning. Come on, which do you like best?'

He picked a heavy, ornately worked cloth in blue and silver and bronze, and when the stallholder released a length from the bolt he draped it across her, from one shoulder to the other, so that it fell in soft folds beneath her face. 'This one,' he said, looking at her, imagining how she'd look with her hair streaming down her back. 'I like this one.' For a moment she seemed to read his mind, see what he was seeing. 'It'll go with your toenails.'

She turned abruptly to the stallholder, made her choices.

'Before going to the museum?' he asked as she waited for it to be packed. She frowned. 'You said you'd go to the weaving centre on Sunday. Are you going to delay your first look at the princess's treasure?'

He sounded doubtful, and Flora knew he was right to be. On her own, she'd have left the weaving centre until her own business was done. But this was her chance to prove that she put Claibourne & Farraday at least on equal footing with her own work.

'This is business,' she said, as if she always put business before academic work. 'I'll need to set up some contacts, arrange for samples to be sent back to London by courier.'

'Then why have you bought all this?'

'I want to see what these look like made up. How they feel. What I need right now is a tailor.' And that was something that wouldn't wait. She looked around as she handed him the parcel. It was heavy, and if he was going to be old-fashioned he might as well be useful. In return she surrendered her hand to his when he reached for it. It meant nothing, after all. Absolutely nothing. 'Thanks for your patience,' she said.

'Not at all. Shopping is clearly very hard work. And you're doing it out of office hours, too. Above and beyond the call of duty.'

'I'll remind you of that remark next year, when women are storming the shops for jackets made from

Saramindan cloth and Claibourne & Farraday are the only place in town to have them.'

'You mean you'll stay on as design consultant when we take over?' he asked.

She looked up at him with a smile. 'Trust me, Bram. It isn't going to happen. You should forget about taking over, accept the inevitable. Just let it go.'

'You're right.'

'Hallelujah!' she cried. 'The man has come to his senses—'

'You're right that this is no place to discuss business. Let's find somewhere to eat and we can talk terms over something exotically ethnic.'

Well, she hadn't for one moment thought he was going to concede that easily. He wasn't even doing her the courtesy of being serious. He was just teasing. She said, 'Over there. That'll do.'

He looked around, expecting to see a restaurant. 'Where?'

'That tailor's shop. It says they do a twenty-four-hour service.'

'But no food?'

'Work first. Eat later.' She crossed the street and he had no choice but to let go or follow her.

He let go...and put his hand to her back, moving closer to ease her through the throng. The imprint of his palm, his fingers, sizzled through the black cloth of her tunic.

'How long is this going to take?'

'Who can say? When you're working, time doesn't matter. But you don't have to stay and watch.' She moved away, putting a few inches of clear space between them. 'There's a bar next door. Why don't you go and get a beer or something?' *Give me some breathing space.* 'I'll come and find you when I'm done here.'

'Contrary to everything you appear to believe, I'm not desperate for alcohol. When you're working, I'm working. Isn't that how it's supposed to be?'

'In theory,' she admitted. 'But you must have been to a tailor, Bram. Why don't you just use your imagination?'

'And have you tell your sister that I was a nine-to-five shadow? Couldn't stand the pace? No way.' He nodded in the direction of an elderly man wearing a traditional sarong, hovering expectantly, waiting for her to notice him. 'Whenever you're ready, Flora.'

She let it go with what she hoped looked like a careless shrug and took her time going through the pattern books with the tailor—matching cloth to styles, linings to cloth, sizing buttons that would be covered with the same cloth. And all the time she was conscious of Bram's gaze following her every move.

It was like a game of chicken…each waiting for the other to back down, say 'enough'.

It would be a cold day in hell before that happened, she promised herself as she submitted to the tailor's tape measure—lifting her arms to be measured around the bust and waist and hips, bending her elbow for the sleeves, turning around so that he could measure across her shoulders, neck to waist, waist to hip. All the time Bram's gaze was almost palpable in the little shop, following every tiny touch of the old tailor's fingers.

It was as if he were the one brushing his fingers against her neck as the tape was run across her shoulders. Touching her wrist. Pushing the tape into her waist.

And her body, famished for a lover's touch, leapt in shocking response, her breasts tightening, a hungry ache settling low in her abdomen in response to a look that was as physical as a caress.

CHAPTER SIX

'I BELIEVE he's finished, Flora.'

'What?'

'I believe the tailor's finished measuring.'

She dragged her mind back to reality. The reality that he was simply bored. And that she should know better. The tailor was nodding and saying something that she finally realised was meant to be 'tomorrow', and she repeated the word, nodding to indicate that she understood.

'Are you done here? Shall we go?'

'Yes. And yes,' she said, eager to escape the confines of the tiny shop, breathe in some fresh air. Outside it was cooler, but the air was heavy and noticeably humid with the slight drop in temperature. It clung damply to her, intimate as a second skin.

Bram paused on the pavement and looked around. 'We could eat over there,' he said, his hand at her back as he indicated a restaurant set back from the street.

'Fine,' she said, moving as if stung. 'Anywhere.'

He turned to her. 'Are you all right?'

'Of course I'm all right,' she snapped.

'We could go back to the hotel if you're tired.'

'Don't fuss, Bram.' Then, 'I'm sorry. I'm just hungry.'

'Oh, right. The low blood sugar. I remember.' But

Bram wasn't convinced. It might have been the street lighting washing the colour from her face, but he didn't think so. For a moment he'd thought she was going to faint. Her voice was sharp enough, though, and maybe food, something to drink and a good night's sleep would fix her up.

The bar was busy, but he found them a couple of seats, organised a table for dinner and returned to Flora with cold drinks and a menu. 'You choose,' she said. 'I need to wash my hands.'

He rose as she left her seat and went in search of the washroom, watching her for a moment. Then, when he was sure she knew where she was going, he sat down.

She wasn't the only one who was feeling the heat. Feeling something. Watching her while the tailor measured her for jackets, he had let his mind follow the tape circling her body, defining her curves, the smallness of her waist. He'd been conscious of every movement. The way the shapeless tunic she wore moved with her, rose and fell as she lifted her arms, momentarily emphasising her breasts. Shoulder to wrist. Nape to waist. Her head moving a little with each measurement. A single curl descending slowly from a comb.

It had been hypnotic, curiously sensual, and even thinking about it stirred something deep in him, something different that he didn't fully comprehend. It was as if a secret was being revealed to him, but in some arcane language. One that he didn't understand.

The waiter came to take their order. It was a relief to think of something other than Flora Claibourne.

*   *   *

Flora washed her hands, splashed her face. She was trembling. For a moment in that hot little room, with the tailor calling out her measurements to his assistant and Bram watching every movement, she had been weak with longing. He'd done that just by looking at her. It was as if she were seventeen all over again. For a moment she clung to the basin. Then slowly and carefully she took all the combs from her hair, brushed it out, and just as slowly, put it up again. Only then did she return to the restaurant and to Bram.

'Are you going to copy those earrings? Is that what you do?'

Flora, who wasn't particularly hungry, had taken out the earrings she'd bought for a closer look while Bram indulged in some sticky pudding. It had been a while since he'd said anything to irritate her. He'd seemed preoccupied—and his mouth had been otherwise engaged. It had given her all the time she'd needed to recover from her momentary weakness.

'You haven't seen any of my designs?' she asked, with an air of mild surprise. It was the nearest she'd get to dignifying his attack with an answer. 'I confess I'm disappointed. I thought you would have been much more thorough in your research. But clearly you stopped at the gossip about my mother. I have to admit it's a lot more entertaining…' She didn't look at him, but picked up one of the pieces and let it hang, catching the light as it turned. 'These are really very attractive. It's a pity that the finish isn't better or I'd consider buying some for the store.'

'Why don't you find the person who makes them

and tell him that?' he suggested. 'If he knew you were keen to buy he might try a little harder to please.'

'Why do you say "him"? It could just as easily be a woman. Or do you discount women in every aspect of business?'

'I wasn't being gender specific, simply using the convention for simplicity.'

She laughed. 'Come off it. You never gave it a second's thought. You just assumed someone who can set up a workshop, produce goods and get them to market has to be a man. It's that Farradaysaurus thing again. Get up to date. We're in the twenty-first century here.'

'Maybe.' Then he grinned. 'But a hundred pounds says I'm right.'

Flora's foreign travels rarely involved luxurious beach resorts. She went to the rural heartlands, where the women traditionally did the work and took their goods to market while the men put the world to rights over the beer their wives had brewed. Saraminda might be different, but she doubted it.

'Done,' she said. It would be a pleasure taking his money, she thought, returning to the earring. 'But you do have a point. Whoever made this is undoubtedly doing the best job possible with the tools to hand. Maybe, with someone to back her, set her up with new equipment, she could achieve quality to match the design.'

'In an ideal world we'd all have such a fairy godmother.'

'The world is what we make it.'

'We? As in Claibourne & Farraday?'

'Why not? There's nothing to stop us from waving a magic wand.' She hadn't actually thought that far ahead, but making such an offer would go a long way towards demonstrating her credentials as a fully paid up member of the Claibourne & Farraday board. And India—delighted that she was taking an interest— would back her judgement. Probably.

Bram half rose as she stood up, good manners so deeply inbred that even when he was being plain rude it was impossible to override them.

'No, don't disturb yourself,' she said. 'Finish your pudding. I won't be long.' And, still holding the ear-rings, she picked up her bag and walked out of the restaurant to search for the stall where she'd bought them.

Bram, ignoring her instruction to stay put, muttered something less than complimentary about women in general and Flora Claibourne in particular as, aban-doning his half-eaten pudding, he tossed down enough notes to pay for their meal twice over before going after her.

She looked around with apparent surprise as he caught up with her at the jewellery stall where she was writing her name, and that of the hotel, in a notepad.

He didn't believe that surprise. She'd known he'd follow her.

'You shouldn't have rushed, Bram,' she said kindly. 'You'll get indigestion.' And she tore the page out of the notebook and handed it to the puzzled stallholder.

'This guy doesn't know what you want.'

Flora jiggled the earrings, did a little mime that even to his untutored eyes suggested someone cutting a design from metal. 'I want to talk to the person who made this,' she said, then pointed to the paper.

His expression remained blank. Bram, his wallet still in hand, took out a fifty-dollar bill and showed it to the man, then pointed to the earring and the paper, making the connection suddenly very interesting. The man's eyes lit up and he nodded vigorously.

'Money—the universal language,' Bram said as he returned the banknote to his wallet.

'It should get someone to come.'

'At least at the hotel there'll be someone who can translate,' he said.

'Right...and then we can do business...'

He glanced up as her voice trailed off and realised that her gaze was fixed to his wallet. He glanced down. She was looking at the photograph.

He snapped the wallet shut, fastened it in his shirt pocket.

'Business?' he asked, and Flora blinked at his sharpness. 'What kind of business?'

'Um...I don't know. At least, not exactly...' It seemed to take her a moment to refocus on where they had been a few minutes earlier, tear her gaze from his pocket. 'I'd like to take a look at the workshop where this was produced. See if there's any way I can help.'

She gave him one of those sideways looks— thoughtful, but keeping her thoughts to herself. Leaving the questions unasked.

'Why?' he asked, wanting to distract her.

She lifted her head a little, her forehead puckering in a frown.

'Why would you care?' he persisted. 'You buy this

kind of jewellery mass produced from a factory, surely?'

'You must be confusing Claibourne & Farraday with some other department store, Bram.'

'Must I?'

'When was the last time you had a good look round?'

'Not recently. And even if I shopped there every week I wouldn't buy this kind of stuff.'

Gradually the conversation was cranked back to the mundane.

'Of course you wouldn't. It's not expensive enough. Not important enough for the kind of women you date.'

He lifted his eyebrows in a *What do you know about it?* look. She twitched her own brows into an *Am I wrong?* response and he let it go.

'This is something a girl would buy for herself, or a friend, or a sister. For fun,' she explained. 'Shopping as entertainment.'

'You'd buy them for India?'

'Not India. She goes for the classic look. I'd buy them for Romana, though. She's younger, funkier. They'd look fabulous on her. We're always looking for interesting stuff for our younger customers.'

'It's a big market?'

'It is if you get it right.'

'But how do you know? How can you tell...?' He stopped, turned to her so that they formed a still island, the crowds parting to go round them, leaving them untouched. 'Put them on.'

'What?'

'Put them on,' he repeated. 'I want to see them in action. I want to see what you see.'

'Now?' she asked. 'Here in the street?'

'It's just a pair of earrings, Flora. I'm not asking you to model underwear.'

For a long moment he thought she was going to tell him to get lost. But then she lifted her shoulders a fraction, passed the earrings to him to hold while she reached up to take the tiny gold studs from her ears, tilting her head first one way then the other as she removed them.

Not underwear, maybe. But this *was* something she would normally do at her dressing table, in the privacy of her bedroom with only a lover to see her.

It lent her movements an unexpected intimacy. As if she were disrobing just for him. And as she dropped the studs into his hand, warm from her body, and re-trieved the silver earrings, her fingertips brushing against his palm, he felt a jolt of unexpected heat—like the opening of an oven door—and caught a glimpse of something beneath the disguise. Something unconsciously sensuous in the way she moved.

For a moment he could scarcely breathe.

'Well?' she said, when he didn't immediately react.

'Give me time.' He snapped his fist shut around the studs and dropped them into his pocket. Then, taking her hand, he headed back towards the Jeep, glancing at her from time to time as the polished metal caught the light.

The earrings emphasised the length of her neck, he thought. Or maybe she was holding her head a little higher to show them off. Or maybe, without something to catch his eye, he just hadn't been looking closely enough. She half turned to check if he was looking, and when she saw that he was lifted her hand self-consciously to her ear. The same gesture she used when touching the combs in her hair. And for the same reason. To break eye contact.

'Leave it,' he said roughly. 'Let it be.' Then, to diffuse the sudden and baffling swell of intensity, 'Tell me again what you plan to do.'

'It's scarcely a plan—little more than an idea.'

'Well, that's perfect. What could be more perfect than for your ''shadow'' to watch it evolve.'

She glanced at him, as if to check that he was being serious. Apparently convinced, she said, 'I'm always coming across small producers like this, who make exciting stuff. Unfortunately it lacks the finish we're looking for. Maybe, thanks to you, we can do something that will help all of us.'

'Thanks to me?'

'You were the one who suggested that whoever makes these is trying as hard as he can. It wouldn't cost much to provide a proper workshop and decent tools. Maybe some training.'

'And this would be funded by Claibourne & Farraday?' he asked, encouraging her to expand on her idea. It sounded just the sort of woolly-minded, do-gooding nonsense that Jordan would want to know about.

'You have to speculate to accumulate. That's the first law of business.' She cast another of those sideways looks in his direction. This time it held just a hint of provocation. 'As a *lawyer*, Bram, I'd expect you to know that.'

He rather enjoyed her little play on words. He didn't much enjoy the message behind it, but had to acknowledge that she was right. He was a corporate lawyer; what did he know about retail trade? Or about what would bring young women flocking into the store to buy for 'fun'?

Not a thing. He and Jordan and Niall were a generation away from any contact with the reality of the department store their ancestor had jointly founded back in the nineteenth century. They weren't interested in the reality. They would sit on the board but they wouldn't concern themselves with the details.

They were only interested in the bigger picture. The financial issues. The value of the real estate they were sitting on. If—when—the moment was right they would realise their assets and sell out to one of the big high street chains looking for a London flagship store.

Once they had control, the Claibournes wouldn't be able to do a thing about it. They'd just have to take their share of the profits and be grateful that the Farraday men weren't swayed by sentiment, only by profit.

They'd never bother with anything minor, like 'fun' earrings. Or the people who made them.

'And the second?' he said, as they wandered through the crowds in the direction of the car.

She stopped, turned and looked up at him. 'Second?'

'If there's a first law of business, then it follows there must be a second.'

'You haven't been listening, Bram. I've been telling you the second law of business from the moment you began shadowing me. You have to get involved. You have to care about the smallest detail because everything has to fit together. The jackets and the earrings will blend perfectly because they have the same origins, but that's only half the picture. What would look good with them? Gathered silk trousers in soft toning colours, perhaps? Strappy high-heeled sandals in soft leather?' She smiled briefly, as if seeing the ensemble in her mind's eye and liking it, then she refocused on him. 'Buy one part of the look and you'll want the rest.'

'That's what you do?' he asked. 'Make sure everything fits?'

'That's India's job, working with the chief buyer who co-ordinates a look throughout the store. I simply provide the inspiration for a style.'

'That's what you call being *involved*?' He forced scorn into his voice to disguise any hint of admiration.

'It's a lot more involved than anything you're planning,' she returned, just a little sharply. And then, with a considerable amount of perception, 'If you take control, will you be taking the easy option and buying costume jewellery from a factory?'

'Suppose you tell me why that's such a bad idea,' he said, opening the car door for her without bothering about whether it would offend her feminist principles. Not even thinking about it.

And she didn't pause to tell him she could manage quite well, thank you very much. She was too busy explaining the difference between a store where everything was mass-produced and one where each item had earned its place in a display on merit.

He wasn't sure which of them was more surprised by her passion.

'Would you like a drink?' he asked as they walked through the entrance to the hotel. 'It's not late.'

'Isn't it?' She looked at her wristwatch and realised it was still short of midnight. 'I can't seem to get my head around what time it is. Okay. In the cause of investigation, I'll try a glass of the local ginger liqueur. Why don't you go through to the bar while I check at Reception to see if there are any messages?'

She spotted the blonde, sitting on a stool at the open-air bar beside the floodlit pool as if waiting for someone who had never arrived. 'You won't be short of company,' she said.

The woman had changed from a silk shirt and trousers to a clinging evening dress, but otherwise she might not have moved all day.

'What happened to the drinks?' Flora asked when she returned from Reception and realised that he hadn't moved.

'I remembered that you want to make an early start tomorrow.' Taking her elbow, he headed in the direction of the bungalow.

At the door to her room, Flora stopped and held out her hand. 'You still have my studs.'

He retrieved them from his pocket and waited while she removed the long silver drops from her ears and held them up for a moment, looking at them rather than at him. 'Did you learn anything?' she asked.

That her skin was cream silk. That long, swinging

earrings were sexy. That she was self-conscious about being looked at.

'Only that they're pretty and that you're probably right. They'll fly out of the shop.'

'You're getting there. I particularly like the bit where you think I'm right.' She took the studs from his palm and replaced them with the earrings she'd worn for him. 'Take them and look at them whenever you doubt it. A souvenir of Saraminda.'

'Thank you.'

'My pleasure. I'll see you tomorrow.'

'Right. You can tell me some more about getting involved,' he said, then realised she was frowning. 'What?'

'I've left the rest of the jewellery I bought in the Jeep. If you'll give me the keys, I'll just slip and get it.'

He had the feeling that offering to go for her would provoke one of those feminist moments, so he handed them over without a word.

Involved! What a joke! She tugged her brush through her hair. She was the last person in the world to tell someone else to get involved in anything. Her own life, personal and business, was an involvement-free zone. She'd made it her business to keep it that way.

She replaced her ear studs. Neat, unobtrusive. Almost invisible. She'd worked hard to be that way. There had been a time when she'd loved making her own earrings. Exotic, eye-catching, joyously vivid. She'd made dozens of pairs, using anything that came to hand. Feathers. Plastic. A box of brightly coloured children's sweets.

Tonight, as Bram's gaze had burned into her neck, it had all come rushing back.

She'd half expected him to reach out, his fingers brushing her neck as he lifted the earring, or touched it, making it swing. She'd made a tiny pair of replica swings once, hoping to provoke exactly that reaction. And the man she had been aiming to provoke had reached out and touched one. Setting it in motion.

She gave a little shiver as she climbed into bed. Some memories were not to be treasured, stored up against the bad days. Some memories caused the bad days and had to be kept locked away in the dark, where they couldn't hurt. She closed her eyes.

And yet as she lay back against the pillows her brain refused to shut down and let her rest. It was bubbling with ideas. She couldn't wait to talk to India and Romana about her idea for sponsoring local craftsmen. Get some feedback from them.

Bram had been cautious on their drive back to the hotel, his legal brain raising all kinds of difficulties in an attempt to fill her mind with doubts. But far from being irritated, she'd been grateful. The company lawyers would undoubtedly do the same, and if she could anticipate their objections it would save a lot of time.

Maybe a charitable trust was the answer.

She would ask Bram about that in the morning. Maybe, as a lawyer, he'd be prepared to be part of it. He had given her the idea and he was a Farraday, after all. She didn't want them taking the store from India, but there was no reason they shouldn't be involved in something like this. It was stupid to be so divided.

There was the fabulous local cloth, too. That had been a real find. And everything she'd seen so far suggested Saraminda was going to be a hot tourist destination once the word got out.

Princess or no princess, this was going to be a productive visit, she decided. And then realised it was the first time all evening that she'd thought about her real reason for visiting the island.

Convincing Bram Farraday Gifford that she was a serious businesswoman was unexpectedly stimulating—exciting. Remembering the way she'd felt as he'd looked at her in the tailor's shop, the way he'd looked at her wearing those earrings, she knew it was more than that. The stimulation, the excitement, had nothing to do with business. Everything to do with the man.

And then she remembered something else. The glimpse of a snapshot. A boy with his dog. Four, five years old, perhaps. With white-blonde hair. The way Bram had shut the wallet when he'd seen her looking...

At that point she gave up trying to sleep, got out of bed and switched on her laptop.

CHAPTER SEVEN

INVOLVED. The word was beginning to haunt him. His private life was barren of involvement on any meaningful level. His business life too. Corporate law wasn't a field that dealt in the personal.

Bram had mocked Flora's 'involvement', believing it to be a sham, yet he was forced to concede that Flora Claibourne was doing more for the success of the store than he ever could—ever would want to.

Her enthusiasm for improving facilities for local artisans had really got to him. She'd been well up to speed on the public relations possibilities of such a venture too. This wasn't simply an altruistic gesture from a woolly-minded woman. It was something he'd want to pursue when the Farradays moved into the boardroom. With Flora.

This was her vision and she should see it through, take the credit. It was a huge company now. They were partners and it was crazy to waste talent this way just because of some old feud. Obviously Jordan would have to step into the number one slot. It was his right...

Right? Should a clause in a partnership agreement drawn up in a different age decide who ran Claibourne & Farraday? Surely they should be considering who was most qualified to make a success of the job? Flora had an instinctive feel for retailing. They could replace her in the boardroom but they'd have to pay someone else to take her place. Except no one could do quite what she did. No else would be so…involved.

Good grief! She'd got him on her side! Ready to go up against Jordan and tell him to think again.

What was it about these sisters?

His cousin Niall—a man frozen in grief, to the despair of his family and friends—had apparently taken one look at the lovely Romana Claibourne and experienced instant meltdown. Even now they were honeymooning in some romantic hideaway.

Not that there was any danger of such a thing happening to him.

He skirted around the moment when he'd draped a length of rich cloth over Flora's shoulders. Sidestepped his reaction to her in the confined space of the tailor's shop when, as the old man had defined her figure with his tape, his attention had been caught, held by the feminine grace in her movements. Tried to shut out the hypnotic swing of the silver earrings brushing against the long curve of her neck, focusing his entire mind on those few square inches of pale skin.

It had been all he could do to stop himself from reaching out to touch it, discover whether it could possibly be as silky smooth as it looked.

It was as if the drabness of the clothes she wore acted as a backdrop against which small delights could shine for those with the wit to notice them—delights that would have been lost against the competition from designer clothes, a stylish haircut.

He flung back the sheet and swung himself from the

bed. Knowing that sleep wouldn't come, he tugged on his shorts, opened the doors and stepped out into the darkness, seeking a breath of cool air from the sea.

The glow of Flora's lamp was spilling out through open doors, suggesting that she was finding sleep hard to come by too. The sight of her sitting at her dressing table, a blue silk robe trailing loosely about her, her hair a dark ripple of shining waves tumbling down her back, all barriers down, brought him to an abrupt halt. And all the images that had been safely in his head were suddenly there, in front of him.

Then she turned and he saw the open laptop on her dressing table, heard the modem dialling up an internet connection, realised what she was doing. Not sleepless, but working. Reassuring her sister that her 'shadow' was being kept tightly to heel. Filling her in on all the gossip.

'Bram? Do you want something? Is anything wrong?'

'Wrong?' He let his gaze drift over her for a moment. 'There's not a thing wrong that I can see.' The only thing wrong was that he wasn't back in his room updating Jordan. But then what could he tell him? That the woman was a mystery. An enigma. That her mouth was full and ripe and needed no enhancement. That when she wore long earrings her neck became a place a man wanted to touch. With his hands, his mouth. That he wanted to wrap himself in her hair. Even as he thought it she caught it up, twisting it onto her head and securing it with a couple of combs.

'Don't…'

She remained poised with her hands raised, the

loose sleeves of her gown sliding down to reveal the pale skin of her arms, waiting for him to finish what he'd started to say.

'You should get rid of the combs,' he said, more harshly than he'd intended.

'Rid of them?'

'Throw them away. Never wear them again.'

'That's your beauty tip for the week, is it?'

He remembered the man who'd told her not to cut her hair. And knew without a doubt that he was the man who'd hurt her. 'I'm sorry. Forget it. It's none of my business.' She shrugged, let it fall and he caught his breath. He had to admit, the bastard was right. It was her best feature. His cousin, however, was unlikely to be impressed with a list of the lady's attributes. He wasn't supposed to be founding a fan club. 'I'm going down to the beach to cool off. I saw your light and wondered if there was a problem, but I can see you're working.'

'No. At least...'

All evening Flora had been experiencing echoes of the past reverberating in her head. The tiny touches to her back, her arm, the concern as he'd taken her hand, the looks designed to make a woman feel beautiful, special, wanted. The opening moves of the mating game. She knew them all by heart. It didn't make them any less potent. For a moment she'd thought he was moving on to the late-night chat. The part where he opened his heart, shared his pain. Recalling the picture in his wallet, she was sure it would be a heartbreaker. And she did want to know...

'I was just going to send India a note to say we'd

arrived safely,' she said, resisting the emotional tug. 'I should have done it earlier.'

'Then don't let me disturb you.' His eyes were in the shadows, his expression unreadable. But his voice was cobweb-soft, stirring the down on her skin like a caress.

'Let you?' she snapped back, fighting the attraction every step of the way. 'How can I stop you? You disturb me simply by breathing.'

'Is that so? Then I'm sorry.'

'I doubt that. Very much.'

'I haven't exactly cornered the market in disturbance. You're about as restful as a wasp nest.' Behind her the laptop pinged to inform her that she'd got an e-mail waiting to be read. 'Your sister is impatient for all your news,' he said. 'You've got a lot to tell her.'

Oh, no... He knew she'd seen the photograph in his wallet. She didn't want him to think she was sending this juicy piece of gossip to her sister. Whatever his secret—and nowhere in India's file had it mentioned that Bram Gifford had a son—she'd respect it. She wanted him to know that, and she turned back to close down the connection.

'Wait, Bram. I'll come with you,' she said. 'This can wait.' But when she turned back, he'd gone.

'Bram?' She crossed to the open door and saw him striding down the path towards the beach, his hair, his shoulders gleaming in the starlight as he walked away from her as fast as he could.

She rubbed the thin film of sweat from her upper lip. He wasn't the only one who needed to cool down. But it wasn't just her body that was overheated. Her imagination was doing a pretty good impression of a pressure cooker about to blow.

Cool down? She frowned. He wouldn't, surely, go into the sea? Swim at night. Alone?

Bram stood at the water's edge, the cooling surf washing around his ankles, hands in his pockets, his thumb flicking against the teeth of Flora's comb.

He'd put the rest of them, with her hairpins, on her night table when he'd left a bottle of water for her. But this one had been in his pocket and he'd hung onto it, knowing somehow that it was a clue to her deepest secrets.

She had secrets, or she wouldn't need all that hair stuff, that touch-me-not force field to keep him at bay. Personal secrets. None of Jordan's business. None of his business. He, more than anyone alive, knew that.

And yet he sorely wanted to know what had driven her behind her armour-plating. Getting hurt was all part of growing up and she didn't seem to be the kind of girl who'd say once was enough. She was stronger than that. It had to have been something shattering.

Yes, well, he knew about that too, and he found himself wishing that he hadn't walked away. That she were with him. Maybe in the still darkness she'd open up, talk to him. Or maybe not. What would it take to shatter that self-control?

He suspected he'd have go deep inside himself, to his own walled-off cell of pain, for the answer. What would it take to make *him* open up and lay bare his own private grief?

Rather than face the question, he shucked off his shorts and walked into the sea.

Flora paused as she reached the beach, brought to a standstill by the sight of Bram momentarily bathed in the light of the rising moon as he walked into the sea.

He was quite beautiful, she thought. And quite stupid. Swimming at night, alone, was completely idiotic.

'Bram…' Her voice, thick, husky, barely reached her own ears, let alone his. Her bare feet sank into the soft sand and she seemed to make no headway against it. 'Bram!' she called again, this time with sufficient volume, but too late. Even as the sound disturbed the still night he disappeared beneath the dark surface of the sea.

She stood for a moment, her hand to her throat, her heart in her mouth. It was an eternity before he re-emerged, further out, his arms dripping phosphorescence as he cut through the still water.

'Idiot,' she whispered as she sank down onto the sand to keep watch, and she would have been hard put to it to choose which of them she was referring to. Bram for swimming alone in the dark. Or herself for wishing she was with him, the cool water lapping against her hot skin, Bram's hand against her back, with nothing between her skin and his other than a cool film of water—rapidly heating up.

It was like being seventeen again. Heart-poundingly in love with the most beautiful man in the world and with only one thing on her mind.

She groaned and lay back on the sand, her arm over

her eyes, before temptation got the better of her and she joined him.

Bram's private demons didn't often get the better of him. He kept a lid on the pain, kept himself too busy to be caught out by quiet moments when thoughts could steal in and take him by surprise.

For a while he swam hard and fast, concentrating on the physical, excluding everything else. But it didn't help.

Wondering about her secrets had stirred up the past, shaken loose his own, and after a while he turned over onto his back and kicked gently for the shore, standing up when he reached the shallows. Then he turned and saw Flora, stretched out on the sand, her arm over her eyes.

For a moment he stood quite still, rooted to the spot by this unexpected revelation of the woman beneath the camouflage. He'd suspected the truth, but now the lightest breeze off the sea was moulding the thin silk of her robe to every contour. Like some ancient statue of a Greek goddess, she was clothed, but nothing was concealed, and she was more, much more than his imagination had suggested.

He moved as quietly as he could in an effort to retrieve his shorts, but without moving her arm, she said, 'That was a very stupid thing to do, Bram,' and he was the one who jumped. 'You could have been eaten by a shark and no one would ever have known what had happened to you.'

'If I'd been eaten by a shark,' he replied, pulling on

his shorts, 'your problems would be over.' He fastened the button at the waist. 'You can open your eyes now.'

'They weren't closed.'

He understood, finally, why women blushed as his skin responded with a quick flush of heat. Not embarrassment in his case...

'Oh, and in answer to the question you asked earlier—skinny-dipping is an arrestable offence in Saraminda.'

'How do you know?'

'I read the guidebook from cover to cover while you were taking your siesta.' She sat up, brushing the sand from her shoulders, then, after a moment's hesitation, took the hand he offered to help her to her feet.

For a moment he continued to hold it. For a moment she let him. Then she reclaimed it to finish shaking the sand from her hair, her robe, and before his eyes her lovely figure disappeared in a swirl of loose silk and the disguise was pretty much back in place.

Too late. He knew it now for what it was.

Only the reason for it still eluded him as, dignity personified, she turned to walk back to the bungalow. The effect was somewhat spoiled by a nocturnal crab, with eyes like red headlamps, hurtling straight towards her in a headlong dive for the ocean.

She jumped about a foot in the air, venting an involuntary little scream, almost landing on the creature in her panic to avoid it, before flinging herself at him with the unrestrained abandon of any woman confronted by a creature with too many legs for comfort.

'It's just a crab, Flora,' he said, absorbing her tremor into his own body, briefly taking full advantage of her momentary weakness, then letting her go before she found her voice and demanded that he did. He just held her arms to keep her steady.

But her voice had apparently deserted her, and as he looked down into her startled face he discovered a dangerous desire to kiss a mouth that was, after all, quite tempting enough without the enhancement of lipstick. A dangerous desire to do a lot more than that. A rush of heat so intense that he was forced to take a step back to keep the fact to himself.

'I take your point about you being more of a danger to the local wildlife than they are to you, though. You nearly crushed the poor thing.'

'Poor nothing,' she croaked. 'It had a six-leg advantage over me.' Then she frowned. 'Or is that eight? How many legs does a crab have?'

'As many as it needs to avoid big-footed bipeds. With blue toenails.'

She pointedly removed her arms from his grasp, then staggered a little in the soft sand.

He caught her hand. It was still trembling. 'Okay, now?'

'I'm just fine!' she declared loudly, betraying her vexation at having made an exhibition of herself.

'Of course you are,' he said. You aren't in the least afraid of...*arthropoda*. Just crabs.'

'It made me jump, that's all.'

Her voice wasn't as steady as it might be either. And, looking down at her flushed cheeks, her full, soft mouth, for a heartbeat he found himself wondering if it was entirely the fault of the crab.

Taking a wilful decision to find out, he tightened

his grip on her hand, hooked his arm around her waist and drew her towards him with a firm insistence that brought her back to him in a single step.

He'd anticipated a little more resistance.

Maybe he'd taken her by surprise, or maybe it was the scent of the sea and the frangipani mingling to fill the air with an undeniable sensuality that seeped into the mind. Now there was nothing but the luscious feel of the silk between his skin and hers. Between her full, sweet breasts and the hammering of his heart.

'Bram...' Her lips parted softly on his name. Warning or plea? He took the risk, holding her close, cupping her head in his palm as he lowered his mouth to hers. In that moment before his lips brushed over hers she sighed his name again, and he had his answer.

Kissing Flora was like rain in the desert. Fresh, sweet, unexpected.

She kissed him as if he were the first man on earth, as if she were the first woman—her lips trembling beneath his, hovering between flight and surrender. Questioning his motives.

He felt her uncertainty. She expected him to lead, to take what he wanted. He was overwhelmed with an unexpected need for her to give freely, and he answered her doubt with his experience, kissing her as if she were truly a sleeping beauty...as if he were waking her after a hundred years...tenderly at first, a chaste salute, holding back the clamour of his body, making no move to touch her more intimately, to deepen his kiss, extend the delicate exploration of his tongue.

Even when she opened her mouth, inviting more,

he held back, inviting a response, not forcing it, knowing that she would beg with her lips as she opened up to the heat of her own desire. Knowing that the longer he made her wait, the stronger would become her need, until nothing would stop her from responding to his own surging arousal.

For a moment they remained locked, still. Then, with a soft groan of frustration, her tongue sought out his, urgent, demanding, in a spectacular meltdown.

He'd thought that she didn't know what her body was for. He was wrong. Her mouth was liquid heat and her body melted against him. And the fact that this was a rare surrender made it all the sweeter.

But all the time his brain was clamouring that he'd won, that he'd evened the score for Jordan, that all he had to do now was pick her up, take her to bed and claim the prize.

His heart responded with disgust that he could be so cold, so calculating.

Flora Claibourne was worth a lot more than that. He'd won nothing. She wasn't playing games.

She was battened down, afraid of being hurt, and only genuine desire would have evoked such a heated response in her. She wasn't surrendering; she was offering him something special. Her heart, her trust.

The notion was so startling, so unexpected that he lifted his head, needing to see, to know what she feeling.

Her face was flushed with desire, but there was something else, something unreadable. Hidden. And just as quickly he found himself wondering whether she'd been truly startled when that crab ran at her.

Whether she was just making use of a heaven-sent opportunity to get close to him. Had this been India Claibourne's plan all along? Forget proving how good they were at running the store. Simple seduction was a lot faster. Niall had gone down like a ninepin.

It would go a long way towards explaining Flora's terrible clothes, the awful hair. If she'd made an effort to look stunning he'd have been on his guard—after what had happened with Niall. But then, when she'd appeared out of the night, swathed in silk, her hair about her shoulders, transformed—

'I think you should go to bed Flora,' he said abruptly.

She took a deep, shuddering breath that might have been relief, or disappointment, or both. For a moment he wanted to sweep her back into his arms and let the rest of the world go hang. Instead he held her briefly, kissed her forehead, and said, 'Thanks for looking out for me.' Then he let her go and stepped back.

For a moment she hesitated, torn between flight and a passion that threatened to set the heavens alight. Then she, too, backed off. 'I'd have done the same for anyone,' she said dismissively, but she rather spoiled the effect by adding, 'You won't go back out there, will you? By yourself?'

'No more swimming…' About to say, Unless you're with me, he reconsidered. '…tonight. I'll see you in the morning.'

'Bram—' He knew what she was going to ask. Why had he kissed her? Why had he stopped?

'Tomorrow, Flora,' he said abruptly. 'We'll talk to-morrow.'

For a moment she didn't move. Only her fingers curled up into tight little fists as she slowly, slowly, gathered herself in and withdrew behind the façade. Then she inclined her head in an oddly formal little gesture.

'Tomorrow,' she repeated, before turning away to walk back to the bungalow, climbing the steps without looking back, shutting the doors behind her.

After a moment the light went out.

Bram remained where he was until he came back down from the rush of desire, coming to terms with this unexpected Flora Claibourne. Not only were the dreary clothes camouflage for a body that in a figure-hugging dress would have turned heads anywhere. But her unemotional exterior hid the simmering core of a volcano.

And her detached amusement over his 'problem' with insects had been just an act to disguise her own feet of clay. None of which helped his campaign to oust her from the board of Claibourne & Farraday. He found himself suddenly laughing at the swift change from a young woman who could coolly dismiss the insect world as of no concern to the shrieking, shaking bundle of femininity who'd thrown herself into his arms. If she'd been acting, she deserved an Academy Award.

Then he lost the grin. It wasn't, unfortunately, her only weakness. She also had an insatiable curiosity which, coupled with an unwillingness to hear the word 'no', could only mean trouble.

She was determined to find that tomb. He sympathised with her curiosity, but some inbuilt sense of caution warned him that they should stay well clear of the place. He didn't believe for a minute that it was about to fall on them, but Dr Myan had some reason for keeping them away—one he didn't want to share.

Bram thought frankness would have been wiser— maybe he should have left Flora to push Dr Myan for a reason. Not that he would have told her. The man was a politician to his fingertips. But continued resistance might have given her pause for thought.

As it was…

As it was, he had a sudden blinding premonition about why she wanted the Jeep keys.

Just how devious could Flora Claibourne be when it came to getting what she wanted?

Devious enough, he decided.

After leaving her by the pool that afternoon he'd stopped by the desk to give them the details of his driving licence for the car hire. Then, passing the shop, he'd decided to see if they stocked a more detailed map of the island.

'We've only got the two that Miss Claibourne bought.'

'Two?' Two. The girl had held them up for him to see. The little tourist map. And a large-scale map produced by the Saraminda Department of Survey. For a moment he had been too shocked to speak. Then he'd said, 'It'll have to be the big one. I'm afraid she spilled a cup of coffee over it. It was completely ruined.' And then, because he'd started getting a very bad feeling about it, 'Could you mark the site of the tomb for her again?'

The girl had become agitated. 'I really shouldn't

have done it. You won't tell anyone, will you?' Then, 'It is just to help her with her article? She knows she mustn't go there?'

'She knows that,' he had assured her. 'But why? What's the problem?'

The girl had given an awkward shrug. 'It isn't a good place, that's all. Please, you will make sure she understands?'

He'd certainly tried. She clearly hadn't been listening.

His gaze fell upon the silver earrings lying on his dressing table and for a moment he touched them, his hand covering them as he remembered the way they'd looked as she'd worn them. Remembered her animation, her enthusiasm. That had been real.

As was her determination.

He'd assumed that once they were at the monkey sanctuary her plan was to talk him into going further into the mountains—just for a look. Quite certain of his ability to stop her, it hadn't bothered him that much, but suddenly he wasn't so sure. Opening up the map, he discovered—not entirely to his surprise—that the tomb was nowhere near the monkey sanctuary. It was in the opposite direction.

Forget the cute little monkeys. She hadn't been planning to waste her time on them. Any more than she was planning to spend the day with him.

Flora had looked out for him. Worried about him. Whatever her motives, he could do no less for her.

Flora muffled the alarm clock she kept beneath her pillow. It was barely light, the sun not yet above the horizon as she eased herself out of bed and with the minimum of noise dressed quickly in the clothes she had lain out ready in her bathroom the night before.

Then, carrying her boots and a light rucksack, she let herself out of the bungalow and headed for the resort lobby.

She brushed her teeth in the luxurious poolside powder room, using the facilities without any risk of disturbing anyone—or alerting Bram to the fact that she was up and about. There was no one about to disturb, only the night duty manager who had a cold bag ready for her, packed with food and cold drinks.

'You're not going on your own?' he asked anxiously.

She'd told him they were going to travel to a beach at the far end of the island—stunningly beautiful, according the guidebook—hence the early start.

'No, Mr Gifford is checking out the Jeep,' she said, fingers metaphorically crossed. 'Oil, water. Man stuff,' she said, masking her nerves with a little joke. 'Thanks for this.'

'Have a nice day,' he said, his customer care training well to the fore. Then he spoiled it by saying, 'Don't wander off the main road, will you? It's easy to get lost.' She smiled reassuringly as she took the cold bag. Then she hurried to the Jeep, stowed the cold bag and, taking a deep breath, got in the driver's seat and grinned.

She would love to be a fly on the wall when Bram discovered she'd gone without him. It was scant repayment for the way he'd hijacked her with that kiss. She was still having problems deciding whether to be grateful that he'd cut it short before it got completely out of hand, or just plain mad that he'd found it so easy.

Clearly grateful was the sensible option, but she'd decide next time she saw him. Her pulse-rate picked a little up at the prospect. He'd be mad enough for both of them.

She changed her mind about being a fly on the wall.

He'd be in a very bad mood when he realised what she'd done, and the way he felt about insects—well, he'd undoubtedly swat a fly.

CHAPTER EIGHT

BRAM was woken by an earthquake.

Not a geological event caused by the slippage of the earth's crust.

It was the kind of door-banging, foot-stomping earthquake that happened when a woman was seriously thwarted. When she'd had her carefully laid plans turned upside down by a man. And when she wanted to be certain that he was in no doubt about the way she was feeling about that.

'You bastard!' His bedroom door was flung open and Flora stormed in without bothering with the formality of a knock or waiting for an invitation. 'You rat!'

Well, he'd asked himself what it would take to blow the lid off the pressure cooker. One answer had kept him awake most of the night. This completed the set.

He lifted his face out of the pillow and turned to take a closer look at the transformation he'd wrought by removing the rotor arm from the Jeep's engine. Or, more accurately, by allowing her to think she'd got away with her escape plan and then jerking her back like a toddler in leading strings.

The unremarkable shade of her eyes had heated up to spark fire, her cheeks were flushed, her mouth dark red.

Her hair was different too: drawn back in a neat

French plait that emphasised her cheekbones. But then the combs were redundant today—a nuisance rather than a prop. After all, she hadn't anticipated company.

He was impressed. Deeply impressed. There was something about an angry woman that was…impressive.

'Where is it? What have you done with it?'

'And good morning to you, Miss Claibourne,' he said. 'If it is morning, which I take leave to doubt.' He reached out to check his watch on the night table, giving himself a moment to catch his breath, recover from the arousing blast of her wake-up call. 'I know you wanted to make an early start, but there's a difference between eager and precipitate.'

'Cut the—'

'What's the matter, Flora?' he asked, before she could tell him exactly what he was supposed to cut. He'd got the point. He rolled onto his side, propping himself up on his elbow and wishing it were later— hours later—and that he'd slept through all of them. 'Couldn't you sleep?'

She glared at him, as if daring him to suggest any reason why she might have had trouble. To even mention the kiss they'd shared. 'I slept just fine, thanks very much. Give me the rotor arm and I'll leave you to continue your lie-in in peace.'

Lie-in? Didn't it have to be past seven o'clock before it could officially be termed a 'lie-in'? He didn't bother to argue the point. 'Someone took your rotor arm?' he asked. She was surprisingly well acquainted with the internal combustion engine, it would seem. 'Now, why would anyone want to do that?'

'Don't play games with me. You knew, didn't you? Last night. All that kissing stuff, all that "see you in the morning", was just a load of hogwash. You *knew*.'

'It's morning and I'm seeing you,' he pointed out. 'As for the kiss...I thought it merited a higher mark than "hogwash". But maybe you're more experienced than me.' If he'd been hell-bent on maximum irritation he couldn't have done a better job. But a man had to do what a man had to do: she might never get this angry again. He still had a lot to learn about Flora Claibourne. He didn't want her retreating behind the armour-plating again. Next time she'd be harder to shift. 'I like your hair that way,' he added, just to pour fuel on the flames.

'I don't give a damn what you like.' Tiger's eyes, he thought. Brown and gold and hot. 'What gives you the right to mess with my plans?'

He eased himself up on the pillow, turning onto his back, grabbing at the sheet as it began to slide to the floor. 'Your plans? And they would be?'

'You know damn well what I had in mind.'

'A little illicit exploring on your own?' he suggested, linking his hands behind his head. 'That's against the rules, Flora. I'm your shadow. Where you go, I go. No secret trips allowed.' Then, 'Why didn't you just ask for another car?'

She was momentarily taken aback, and he knew she hadn't even thought about it. She'd been too mad to think. 'How do you know I didn't?'

'Because you're angry about the rotor arm, not about the fact that I put a block on that escape route too.'

'You did what? How? When? How did you know?'

'I'm a lawyer. I can spot a lie at twenty paces.'

'I didn't—'

'And I went to see your friendly shopkeeper. She sold me a map exactly like the one she sold you—even marked the site of the tomb for me after I explained how you'd spilled coffee over yours—'

Flora's mouth dropped open. 'Excuse me? Who's the one telling lies here?'

'I told her I didn't think you'd remember exactly where it was.'

'Great.' She threw up her hands. 'I'm not only a mendacious female, but I'm one with the memory span of a goldfish.'

'And last night, right after I removed the rotor arm from the Jeep, I made a point of asking the receptionist to put a note on the computer to confirm any changes in car hire arrangements personally with me.'

'I might sue, Bram. You—the hotel… *I* hired that Jeep. It was paid for with *my* credit card—'

'I know. It's appalling,' he offered, with mock sincerity. 'But you're not in London now. Saraminda is a place where men run things.'

'And women just run to do their bidding?' She looked at him from under those long lashes, thoughtful rather than flirtatious. 'I have to hand it to you. You're smart. And you're thorough.'

Surely she wasn't going to switch from berating him to flattery? On the point of suggesting she forget about a pile of old ruins and get back into bed—his bed—common sense came to his rescue. 'Thorough is my middle name.'

'No, it's not, it's Farraday.' She shrugged. 'Same thing, I guess,' she said, reaching up to fiddle with her hair before realising that she had nothing to fiddle with. 'In the event the block on the car hire was unnecessary. The guy in Reception was concerned that I might be going off on my own so I said you were in the Jeep. If I'd made a fuss he'd have seen you weren't there. As you said, this is a man's world and I'm sure he would have checked with you.' She pulled a face. 'Men stick together, don't they?'

'Not always. But in this instance I suspect your instincts are right.' He sat forward. 'But only in this instance. Hasn't it occurred to you that when four different people—no matter what their sex—tell you that what you're doing is a mistake, it might be time to start listening?'

'Four?'

'The girl in the shop asked me to remind you that the tomb "isn't a good place"—that you mustn't under any circumstances go there. Consider yourself reminded.'

'All that occurs to me,' she replied, ignoring the warning, 'is that something stinks. That Tipi Myan has something to hide.'

'On that, at least, we can agree.'

'I'm going to find out what's going on, Bram. You won't stop me.'

He'd been afraid of that. But there was an up-side to every situation. 'Why don't you organise some coffee while I take a shower? Then we'll discuss the situation in an open and frank exchange of views.'

She opened her mouth—presumably to tell him to

get his own coffee, give or take a few expletives—but before she could say anything, he flung back the sheet, swung his legs over the edge of bed and stood up.

She didn't hang around to argue.

Bram grinned at her retreating back, but he wasn't underestimating her determination. He retrieved the rotor arm from beneath his pillow and took it with him into the bathroom.

Flora phoned for coffee. Then returned to Bram's room under cover of the noise of the shower for a quick look for the rotor arm. Her search was hampered by her imagination, which seemed more interested in what was happening on the far side of the bathroom door. Then the water stopped and she scooted quickly back to the sitting room and called Room Service a second time to ask for croissants and juice.

It was clear that she wasn't going anywhere in a hurry and she'd been awake long enough for breakfast to sound attractive.

Breakfast and Bram arrived together. Of the two, she thought Bram looked more appetising in a long-sleeved chambray shirt, cuffs turned back to his elbows so that the low slanting sun glinted off the gold hair on his forearms, casual trousers and a pair of soft desert shoes. Not exactly equipped for a jungle trek, but since they weren't actually going on a jungle trek it was close enough.

Neither of them spoke while the waiter laid out the food on the small veranda table. Bram signed the chit while Flora sat at the table and poured the coffee.

'So,' she said, passing a cup to him, 'I intend to go

and take a look at the tomb of the "lost princess" today. Discuss.'

Bram had had plenty of time to think about his answer while he was under the shower. And he knew that if she was determined enough nothing he could do—short of handcuffing her to the bed—would prevent her from doing exactly as she said. He didn't dwell on that idea for too long for fear that it might become irresistible.

What kept hammering at him was the way he'd felt last night. The certainty that he had everything to gain from becoming her ally, her friend. Until he'd kissed her, that had seemed about as likely as hell freezing over. It still might be.

But as he'd stood beneath the cold needle spray of the shower he'd asked himself just how far he was prepared to go to break down the barrier she had erected between herself and the world.

Not the physical barrier. That had been blown away. Even now as they sat there, pretending not to think about it, the air was thick with sexuality. It was simmering beneath the surface, threatening to boil over.

It wasn't enough. Not now. That sex would be hot and exciting and new with Flora Claibourne he did not doubt. But she would still be keeping her secrets behind that barrier.

So. How far would he go? How much of himself would he lay open to her scorn, her judgement?

The answer, it seemed, was that if Flora Claibourne could be brought to a point where she would begin to trust him then it was worth any amount of risk.

He didn't say any of that. Instead he joined her at

the table, moving the chair slightly so that he was sitting opposite her, and said, 'There's not much to discuss. Apparently nothing will stop you from taking off into the forest, with me or without me. If you're really intent on taking this trip, I'll have to come with you.'

'Excuse me?' she asked, not exactly overwhelmed with gratitude at his apparent change of heart.

He'd have been wary in her shoes.

'Did you say you'll come with me?'

'Someone has to keep you out of trouble.'

'You're such a gentleman, Bram. How could I possibly refuse an offer like that?'

'Don't even try. It's the best you're going to get. But, since we have no idea what the problem is, we'll need to take sensible precautions.'

'I've got food,' she told him. 'And plenty of water.'

'Well, that's a start. But we'll need more than food. And a compass.'

'It was a dead give-away, wasn't it?'

'That and the ''eureka'' smile,' he admitted, reaching for a croissant. Flora was like a greyhound in the slips, almost trembling in her eagerness to be off, but he wasn't going anywhere until they'd sorted out the ground rules. 'Have one of these; they're really good.'

She hesitated for a moment, her appetite now subservient to her eagerness to get going. But, since he wasn't about to leap up and go rushing off without thinking things through, she took one and began pulling it to pieces.

'I've got a torch,' she offered. 'I brought it with me.'

'Proper little Girl Guide, aren't you?' he said, teasing her. She shrugged, but he saw she was close enough to a smile as made no difference. And why not? She'd got her own way. There was nothing like getting her own way to make a woman smile. There was nothing like a woman's smile to make a man want to move mountains for her.

'And we've got two maps,' she pointed out. 'Just in case we lose one.'

She even felt confident enough to joke about it.

'Or in the event that we get seriously careless with the coffee,' he agreed. 'Although I was thinking more along the lines of telling someone where we're going—just in case we don't come back.'

'Oh, cheers.'

'And saying that if I think it's too dangerous to go on, you'll listen.'

'Right,' she said. Far too quickly.

'How do you suppose that girl in the shop knows where the tomb is?' he asked. 'Considering it's supposed to be such a big secret.'

'You made the point yourself that when two people know something it's no longer a secret.'

'Perhaps I was exaggerating,' he admitted. Two people *could* keep a secret when for one of them it was more important than life itself and the other had no one to share the burden. 'And a lot more than two people have to know about this.' He frowned. 'From what you said, though, I'd assumed it was deep in the interior. It's only a half a dozen miles from the coast.'

'That was the impression I was given. But then,

Saraminda is a small island. In some places, six miles *is* deep in the interior.'

'You're sure it's the right place?' Given the choice, he'd still rather not poke around in a place where an autocratic government had made it plain they didn't want him to go. 'The girl in the shop might just have been telling you what she thought you wanted to hear.'

'That's always a possibility, but I told her I was writing about the treasure and she appeared to know all about it.'

'But she said it wasn't a "good" place. That's a curious way of putting it, don't you think?'

'Maybe it's a language thing. A lot of people are superstitious about disturbing burials.'

'You told her that you weren't going there. That you just wanted the information for your article.'

'You two did have a nice visit.' Her mouth twitched in the promise of a smile. *Move mountains, cross oceans...* 'Okay, so she was worried about telling me. I distracted her by offering to sign the books she had on display.'

'You do a very nice line in distraction, Miss Claibourne.'

Her eyes softened in response to the sudden thickness of his voice. 'You're not exactly a slouch in that department yourself, Mr Gifford.'

He leaned forward, took her chin in his hand and rubbed his thumb over her mouth. 'If you're referring to the fact that I kissed you—that was not a distraction. It was a promise.'

The quick flush that heated her cheeks provoked a swift response deep within him, but she leapt to her

feet—whether from her eagerness to be off or to put
some clear space between them, he was undecided.

'If you've finished your breakfast, can we go?' she
asked eagerly, as if she was reading his mind.

He wasn't entirely convinced, but at least she'd
stopped pretending to be Miss Cool, which was about
as much as he could take and still keep a clear head.

It was unbelievably hot.

The drive along the coast road was wonderful. They
didn't use the Jeep's air-conditioning, but simply
opened the windows and enjoyed the light breeze coming off the ocean, the glimpses of small, deserted
coves set along the rocky shoreline on one side of the
road. On the other, the dramatically mountainous interior rose sharply above the narrow belt of terraced
farmland.

They agreed that it was magic. That it was going to
be a sensational new holiday destination. It was all
incredibly polite and civilised. And when Bram
stopped so that she could take photographs for the
travel department, they kept a clear foot of space between them by tacit agreement.

Even so, that 'promise' seemed to arc through the
space between them. Primitive, hot. All the more intense for being unspoken.

Once they turned off the road, though, the heat became a reality.

At first the track took them through small traditional
villages, where children stared at them as if they were
beings from another planet and chickens scattered before their wheels. But their destination lay higher up

the slopes and gradually civilisation was left behind. Along with the fresh breeze.

They drove as far as possible, but when the track got too narrow, too steep, they continued on foot, carrying only water and some food. The path had been recently used, and was easy enough to follow, but the forest seemed to press in on them and the air was thick with moisture.

'According to the map, it can't be much further,' Bram said, when they paused to take a drink at a point where the ground fell away steeply and there was an unexpected blast of fresh air. 'And if I were to build a lasting monument to someone great, this is the place I'd choose.'

Flora unfastened the third button of her shirt, flapping the two edges to encourage the cool air to circulate over her skin. 'It would make a great site for Tipi's eco lodge,' she agreed. 'Just look at those orchids…' She took her camera from her bag to take some photographs. The motor wind of her camera disturbed a small flock of brightly coloured birds that rose noisily from the trees as she used up the last of the roll. A huge butterfly drifted past.

'He's right about it being a naturalists' heaven,' she said, dropping the film in the small rucksack she'd loaded up with essentials and slotting a fresh roll into her camera. Bram didn't answer and she looked around.

'Bram?' He'd disappeared. Gone. 'Bram!' she yelled.

'Up here.' At the sound of his voice she swung round and looked up.

For a moment she couldn't see him. Then she caught a telltale glimpse of blue chambray a few feet above her and saw that he'd pushed his way up the hillside through the thick vegetation. He was just yards away, yet almost invisible.

And the possibilities provided by exotic birds and butterflies the size of hang-gliders gave way to less pleasant thoughts about the ecological downside of this demi-Eden: insects, snakes, spiders the size of dinner plates.

Then, remembering her proud boast—so unfortunately undermined by that crab—she pushed all thoughts of such things from her mind and scrambled up after him.

He turned, reached out a hand to pull her up beside him. About to remind him that this place was supposed to be dangerous, that they should stick together—which considering her earlier intention to come here alone was a touch ironic—she stopped, blinked, for a moment unable to take in the magnitude of what stood before her. Then her eyes refocused to accommodate the scale of what she was looking at. 'Oh, good grief...'

The entrance was nothing more than a natural split in the rock face of a towering cliff. She held onto her straw hat as she tipped her head back and looked up at the wall. Under normal circumstances, their gaze might have passed over it a thousand times and they still would never have seen it for what it was. But, although fresh growth was quickly re-invading the cliff-face, it had quite recently been partially cleared to reveal deep, ancient carving. She took a step back, trying to work out what it was. And another. It was a two-headed bird, something akin to a raven, she thought, wings spread protectively around the entrance. It was vivid, almost alive, and it made the tiny hairs on the back of her neck prickle.

'It's awesome,' she said.

'In the full sense of the word,' he agreed. 'Majestic. Powerful. Intended to induce a state of wonder. Or fear.'

It was all of those things, and she shivered, no longer hot. 'The scale of it is quite terrifying.' Then, 'I'd never have found it on my own. It's—what?— twenty feet from the path, and no one would ever know it was here.'

'With creepers growing right up to it, it would have been invisible.'

'What made you look here?'

He turned and looked across at the view that, only fifteen or so feet above the path, stretched endlessly to the ocean. 'That. It seemed…appropriate.'

'Yes. It's absolutely perfect.'

'Perfect,' he agreed, looking down at her. 'And awesome. Do you think that's the problem the Saramindans have with it? A folk memory of the place as somewhere alien? Off-limits?'

'Maybe.' She sounded doubtful. And yet, despite her own immediate reaction, she knew there was nothing to fear.

'Imagine being here, hacking away centuries' growth of creepers to get a better look, and then there's another minor earth tremor.'

'Another one?'

'This part of the world is geologically very active. Something brought that down.' He indicated a huge piece of rockface that had sheared away and fallen to the ground. The forest was quickly closing in on it, but it had once been part of the raven's wing. 'It wouldn't have to be a very big tremor. Just enough to suggest the gods were angry.' He shrugged, leaving the rest to her imagination.

'The curious weren't too scared to help themselves to the princess's gold,' she pointed out as she gathered herself and began to take the pictures she'd come for.

'Maybe they already had it.' He walked towards the edge of the massive façade, where the ground fell sharply, leaving freshly exposed earth and roots. 'The ground over here appears to have been eroded by rainwater. It's undermined this side of the tomb and there's been quite a large rockfall. Maybe they were coming back for another look.'

'So that's it? Mystery solved?'

'Up to a point.' He shrugged. 'I think it would take more than this to scare off Tipi Myan, but there's no sign of any engineering work to underpin the structure.' He looked round at her. 'Are you going inside?'

The entrance was not inviting. 'Is it safe?'

'I'm not an engineer, Flora. You'll get no guarantees from me.'

She would get nothing from Bram Gifford and his promises except trouble, she decided. But his doubt put steel into her backbone. Bram hadn't wanted to come here in the first place, she reminded herself. But she'd been proved right. There was nothing to frighten them but the bogeymen of their imaginations. Hers was working full time, but she refused to wimp out now.

'Your considered opinion will do,' she replied, not looking at him. 'You're a man,' she said. 'You must have one.'

'Don't do that, Flora.'

She blinked at the sudden sharpness in his voice. 'What?' He didn't answer. 'What am I doing?'

'You're treating me like the enemy again. I'm here. I'm with you.' For a moment their gaze locked. 'For you, not against you. If you want to look inside I'll come with you.'

Flora felt as if the ground were crumbling beneath her feet. As if, like the cliff-face before them, the foundations upon which she lived her life were being undermined by Bram Gifford.

First he had taken her hand, and she had not pulled away—sure that she was the stronger, that he could never slip beneath her guard. Too late, she'd learned that she was not immune to the touch of the man's hand, a certain look in his eyes, the hot lick of desire.

Worse, she'd found herself worrying about him, caring that he was safe. He'd seen that, used that, kissing her with a sweetness that was designed to turn her head, make her forget that they were rivals. That they were both after the same prize.

And she'd forgotten.

Now...now...she didn't know what he was doing. She just knew that, more than anything else, she wanted him beside her when she stepped into the dark.

As if he could read her mind, he said, 'All you have

to do is trust me, Flora. All you have to do is ask. Anything.'

The forest seemed to hold its breath, waiting for her to speak.

She should be standing firm. She had been her own woman for a long time. On her own. Needing no one. Until now. She looked up at the massive façade. It was awesome. But she wasn't backing away from it. She wouldn't back away from Bram, either.

'Will you come with me?' she whispered hoarsely. 'Give me your hand.'

He reached out to her and, with her heart beating in her mouth, she lifted her hand and placed it in his. He gripped it firmly for a moment, then said, 'It'll probably be all right as long as we don't breathe too hard.'

'Don't breathe too hard,' she repeated in a voice that was little more than a whisper. It still sounded too loud in the quiet of the ruins. 'Right.'

He squeezed her hand. 'Ready?'

Was she? Ready to step into the unknown? Take a risk?

She took a deep breath, switched on her torch. 'Ready,' she affirmed. Then, as they stepped together into the dark, she turned to him and said, 'Anything?'

CHAPTER NINE

'ANYTHING?' Bram repeated.

'You said I could ask anything.' The beam of her torch swept shakily across the stone floor, littered with the debris of ages. At the far end a vast slab of stone lay tilted, where the earth had been undermined and fallen away. On the opposite wall some elaborate design had been chiselled into the rockface. 'Did you mean it when you said I could ask you anything? Or did you mean that I could ask anything of you?'

He'd thought she hadn't caught the invitation he'd tossed into the conversation. It seemed that he was mistaken. She'd been listening to every word.

'What would you like it to mean?' he asked.

She didn't immediately answer, instead concentrating on widening the torch beam to reveal the whole of the rock wall facing them. Chiselled out of the living rock was a portrait of a woman seated upon a throne, her long hair rippling in tiny formalised waves over her naked breasts. Flora went up close, her fingers tracing the details of the stonemason's art. Intricate carvings that depicted a diadem upon her head, the jewels with which the mason had decorated her arms, ankles, throat. 'It's real,' she whispered.

'Real?'

'I was beginning to think that Tipi had invented the whole thing to get some publicity for the tourist industry. He used to be Minister of Tourism…I thought maybe they'd found some old ruins and he'd brought some old jewels to pass off as grave goods.' She turned to him. 'He wouldn't be the first. Not all that gold at Troy came out of the ground. Schliemann bought most of that stuff. He used to dress his wife up as Helen, like in the famous photograph, just to make his discovery seem more impressive. But this is the real thing.'

'It's incredible.' For a moment Bram had been too stunned to say anything. Then he, too, reached out to touch the face of the 'lost princess'. 'That could be you, Flora.' She turned to him. 'With your hair loose, a centuries-old crown on your head.' Her profile gleamed in the soft spillage of light from the torch and he reached out, touched her throat. 'Ropes of pearls about your throat…precious stones…'

He felt her swallow beneath his hand. 'Don't be foolish. I don't look like that.'

'You are her living image.' He turned to her, laid his hands gently over her face, closed his eyes. 'Brows,' he said, outlining them with his fingers. 'Nose…' He brushed it with his thumbs. 'Mouth…' He didn't need to see her mouth, he knew it intimately. How it looked before he kissed her. How it felt. Full, soft and warm. He didn't need his eyes, he had his mind. It was all there. The sudden shy smile, the quick flare of her unexpected response to him. The slow, melting, surrender. 'You share the same strong features.'

She drew back slightly. Putting an inch of space

between them. 'That's just a polite way of saying I have a big nose,' she said.

He opened his eyes. 'If I thought you had a big nose I'd say so. On anyone else it might be big. On you, it's a perfect fit.' He reached for her plait, removed the band. She made another move to distance herself, but he said, 'Be still now. Let me do this. Then I'll take a photograph of you and the princess, so that you can see for yourself.' And as he began to slowly unravel her hair he said, 'Was there something you wanted to ask me, Flora?'

She was perfectly still as, slowly and carefully, he teased out the windblown plait. Scarcely breathing. Well, that made two of them. 'It's personal, not about the store,' she said, half in question.

They were barely touching. His sleeve skimmed her cheek as he reached around to loosen the tight French plait. His fingers grazed her neck, shivering over her skin. The heavier cloth of his shirt brushed against the fine linen of hers and he felt her nipples tighten, reach for him, begging him to touch them. But he just kept working at her hair.

'Ask what you want, Flora.'

'I just…I wanted to ask you if you've ever been in love.'

It wasn't the question he'd expected. 'I don't know what love is.'

'I knew you wouldn't answer,' she said, letting the torch beam wander over the walls as she breathed out.

He reached out, caught her wrist and turned the light back on the richly carved relief of the princess, stared at it for a moment. 'That's what they've got in the museum? They buried her jewels and crown with her?'

'I imagine so.' Her voice was pert, dismissive.

'Did Tipi Myan say the tomb was decorated?'

'Are you kidding? He must have known that if he'd told me about this nothing would have kept me away.' Then, 'Are you any the wiser as to why he would want to keep me away?' she asked. In the darkness, without the brisk careless gesture, the bright smile to back it up, her voice betrayed her. It told him that she was angry. Not with him, but with herself for believing that he was serious.

'I once thought I was in love,' he said, reclaiming her attention. 'It seemed like love, for a while.'

'What happened?'

'Nothing. We had two months together. Then one day she kissed me and said she had to leave. That it was over.'

'Did you ask her to stay? To marry you?' The question came out in a rush. As if she hated herself for asking, but had to know.

He smiled. It *was* going to be the question he had been expecting, then. She was just going the long way round to get there. Testing his 'anything' promise to the limits. 'I wanted her to stay. And I asked her to marry me,' he confirmed.

'Because she was pregnant?'

'No. I didn't ask her then. That was years later. Long after I'd realised that what I'd thought was love was something quite different. Infatuation on my part...and on hers...well, something else.'

He'd asked himself the question—what would it

take for him to open his heart? And he had his answer. The need to share heart and soul with another person. Someone who had reached out of the darkness and lit him up with an inner warmth, a memory of innocent love that asked nothing, gave all.

'I asked her to marry me on the day I walked into the garden of an embassy in London, saw a small boy playing with the ambassador's wife. And discovered, by the merest chance, that I had a five-year-old son.'

'But...he could have been...' Her voice faltered. 'No.'

'No. You saw the photograph. The reality was...' He paused. 'There was no doubt in my mind. It was like looking at a photograph of myself when I was small.'

He was right about the dark, he thought. This wasn't a moonlit beach, but it was a place full of mystery. Full of secrets. And he'd finally found someone who understood secrets. Someone with whom he wanted to share the biggest secret in the world.

And in the near dark, without the visual clues, his other senses were straining to fill the gaps. He heard the tiny intake of breath that betrayed her shock. Seemed to feel a wave of something warm, empathetic, wash over him.

'You didn't know until then? She hadn't told you?'

He spread her hair out in his hands. Where it had been plaited it was fixed in little waves, like those of the princess watching over them. He hungered to strip away her shirt, see her hair lying over her breasts, but not here. That would wait. Instead he divided it into two and brought it forward, to match the carving on the wall.

'I was right,' he said. 'You could be sisters. Or mother and daughter. I don't believe she was just a princess. I'm sure that she must have been a queen.' He frowned. 'Can you hear something?'

They listened. There was a slight rustling. 'It's the leaves outside,' she said impatiently. 'Bram...' She leaned towards him, encouraging him to answer her.

'No, Flora, I didn't know. She never told me,' he confirmed. 'But then I was never supposed to find out. When we met she was a wealthy woman with a need. I was doing a gap year after university, working my way round France, improving my French so that I could specialise in European law. She would never have expected the waiter she'd picked out—and picked up—in a Marseilles café to be advising an ambassador on English corporate law six years later. Walking into her garden to join his family for afternoon tea.' She reached out, covered his hand with her own.

'She *chose* you? To give her a baby? That was her need?'

Flora was quick, clever. She needed no explanations. 'She didn't tell me what she wanted. I thought she just wanted me. And I was utterly bowled over by this sad, lovely woman who seemed so alone. She was, of course. She was a long way from home in a place where no one would know her. No one would remember her. And the sorrow, at least, was not faked. Nor the pleasure, I hope. She picked me for my height and my colouring. And just a little bit for me, I have to believe.'

'How could she do that?'

'For love, she said. She tried to explain, to show me how it was for her, when we met later. Her husband—the ambassador—was an aristocrat whose family had run out of heirs. Time was running out for them. She couldn't use a clinic for donation—they'd want medical records, details that she couldn't give. And since the child would not be her husband's genetically, his right to inherit the title, the land, would be challenged by distant cousins so far removed as to be total strangers. There is a lot to inherit. So she took the only course she felt was open to her.'

'He knew what she was doing?'

'He must have suspected, but they never spoke of it. She begged me not to tell him who I was. He loved his son—'

'But he was *your* son!'

'What was I to do, Flora? Turn the child's life upside down? Demand my rights? Destroy three lives?'

'Three?'

'They were good people.'

She uttered a tiny dismissive sound.

'Despair will drive the kindest people to do desperate things. And they loved him so much. I sat and watched this man play with my son and inside I was raging, but only because I had no right to love him that way.'

'But you still asked her to marry you? To divorce her husband and marry you?'

'I had to try. She only agreed to meet me because

she was afraid of what I might do. I raged, I threatened, I demanded she leave her husband and marry me. Finally, I begged. She didn't say anything. She just let me say every hurtful thing I could lay my tongue to, waiting until I had said it all. Waiting for me to accept the truth. That biologically John might be my child, but in every way that was important he was her husband's son.'

'John? His name is John?'

'That's the English version of his name. They don't call him that.'

Bram drew a deep breath. He'd known all this for a long time, accepted it even, but finally telling someone made it all seem so much clearer. 'I wasn't there when he was born, or when he first smiled. It wasn't me who held his hand as he took his first steps, or sat with him in the night when he was sick.' Explaining it to Flora was like a release. The guilt eased. 'That's what a father is, Flora. He was a happy little boy, and if I'd demanded my rights, blood tests, all that would have been wiped away.'

She held his hand, telling him by touch that she understood. That he had been right. 'Does anyone else know?'

'Who would I tell? What point would there have been telling my parents that they had a grandchild they could never know? Making them as miserable as I was? He was a happy child; now he's a happy young man. He'll be fourteen this year. If he ever needs me, I'll be there for him. The best part of me hopes he never will.'

Her fingers slipped from his and she reached up to

touch his cheek. Softly wipe away tears he'd been unaware of shedding. And for a moment she held him, her arms about him.

'You said you don't know what love is, Bram, but you're so wrong. Letting go was the perfect act of love. Thank you for telling me.' She looked up. 'For trusting me.'

'I believe it's time we trusted one another, instead of fighting.'

'Are we talking personally, here, or professionally?'

'Both.' He felt rather than saw her nod. 'Have you seen enough?' he asked, lifting his head. There was a soft whispering noise above them. Wind, leaves—it still lifted the tiny hairs on the back of his neck. 'I'd like to get out of here.'

'I'll just take some photographs. Will you take the torch, shine it on the wall so that I can see what I'm taking pictures of? Then maybe we should take our picnic down to one of those beaches.'

'I didn't bring a swimsuit with me.'

'Neither did I.'

'You're quite determined to get us both locked up, Flora Claibourne.'

'I don't know about both of us. I'm sure India would be delighted if I could get *you* locked up.'

He laughed, the sound echoing back from the high walls. But there was more than laughter in the sound. The rustling grew louder. It was above them, around them, the air was stirring, and suddenly he knew what it was. 'Flora!' he warned as she raised her camera to take a picture. 'Don't!'

The flash was blinding in the dark. Neither of them

could see. But he reached out anyway and, finding her arm, dragged her with him towards the entrance. 'I haven't finished,' she complained.

He didn't stop to argue, but bundled her out into the open, where they stood blinking for a moment in the light.

'What on earth—?'

'Bats,' he said. Even as he said the word small dark shapes began to emerge from the entrance to the tomb. Just a few at first, but behind them the tomb was filled with the whirring of wings as the disturbed creatures began to drop from the roof, whirling faster and faster, like angry bees, and then they began to pour out of the entrance like black smoke.

He saw her face, her mouth working in sheer terror, and then she tore free and began to run.

'Flora! Wait!'

Flora didn't stop to listen to reason. Spiders were bad. Snakes were terrifying, but bats... She flung her arms over her head, terrified that they would get tangled in her hair. Everyone told her that it didn't happen, that it was just nonsense, but it made no difference. The crab had startled her. This was real terror.

'Flora! It's all right...' As he reached for her, tried to hold her, she lashed out and ran for dear life back down the path towards the Jeep. 'Look out!'

Too late. She staggered and went down as the path dipped suddenly, dropping onto her knees. But nothing, not even pain, was going to stop her. She staggered to her feet, her arms still around her head, running blindly, but this time she was brought up sharply as Bram grabbed the back of her shirt. For a moment she continued to struggle and there was an ominous ripping sound.

'Be still.' The sudden sharpness in his voice finally got through to her, and as she hovered between flight and collapse he turned her into his body and held her tight. 'I won't let anything hurt you,' he said, stroking her hair, kissing it. 'You're safe.' And he kept saying it over and over. Holding her close, telling her over and over again that she was safe.

Eventually she heard him. Believed him. Slumped against him. 'I'm sorry,' she said, bunching his shirtfront in her hands, mumbling into his chest. 'I'm so sorry. I just panicked.'

'I know.'

She looked up, suddenly more afraid that he was laughing at her than of the bats. 'It's just bats,' she said, trying to retrieve a little dignity.

He dropped a kiss on her mouth as if it was the most natural thing in the world. 'Bats and crabs,' he said, his mouth lifting at the corner in something very like a smile.

But he wasn't mocking her. Just teasing a little. And she discovered that being teased by Bram made her feel great.

'Tell me…just so I can be ready…what you'll do if you meet something really dangerous? A snake, or a spider the size of a dinner plate.' She moaned. 'Right. Well, I guess we know exactly how you feel about creepy-crawlies. Scared to death.'

'I'm not,' she protested. Then, with a tiny shrug, 'At least, not in theory.'

'I'm not sure that theory counts.'

'No.' Then, 'I'm okay with mice.'

'Sugar ones?'

'No, honestly!' She pulled back, then winced as she put her weight onto her left leg and grabbed at him for support. He took one look at the torn knees of her trousers and didn't bother to ask her whether she needed help. He just picked her up and began to carry her back to the Jeep.

About to protest at such high-handedness, Flora changed her mind and instead put her arms around his neck, laid her head against his chest and listened to the slow, steady thud of his heart as he held her safe.

Once they reached the Jeep, Bram handed her a bottle of water, and while she was taking a drink he found the first aid box and gently cleaned up her knees with antiseptic wipes. 'This one is a bit swollen,' he said. She flexed it and winced. 'How bad is it? Do you want to go to the hospital in Minda?'

She shook her head. 'I won't be running a marathon for a week or so, but it'll be fine if I keep my weight off it for a day or two.'

He glanced up. 'You run marathons?'

'It was just a figure of speech, Bram.' Then she realised he was grinning. She handed him the water bottle. 'Here, occupy your mouth with that.' Then, as he tilted his head to take a long drink and she didn't have to look him in the eyes, she said, 'Thank you, Bram.' She made a vague gesture in the direction of the tomb. 'For getting me out of there. Dealing with my hysterics.'

'No problem.' He straightened and she was looking

straight up into his eyes for a long moment. They were both remembering how it had been before she'd run in terror. Then, 'Okay, now?' he asked briskly. 'Heart-rate back to normal?'

Not exactly, she thought.

Her heart-rate was giving her considerable trouble.

'Not exactly,' she said aloud. 'To tell you the truth, I'm feeling pretty stupid. I mean I *know* bats are harmless. In theory.'

'It wasn't just you. The hairs on my neck were beginning to stand on end back there. I can't say I'm sorry to be out of that place.'

'That's sweet of you to say so, but—'

'I'm many things, Flora. Sweet isn't one of them.'

No. And he was probably busy compiling a list of her own shortcomings right now. A reckless disregard for her safety. Hysterics. Jordan Farraday would be proud of him. She shivered again. 'I suppose the bats might explain why the locals think it's spooky,' she said.

'It might. It doesn't explain why Tipi Myan is so keen to keep you away, though.'

'Unless the bats are a rare, endangered species and must not be disturbed.'

'He would have told you that. No, I'm sure there's something else going on, and if you don't mind I think we'll get out of here while the going's good,' he said, handing back the water bottle before easing her legs over the seat and closing the Jeep door. Then he climbed in beside her and slid the key into the ignition.

'Bram...' He glanced at her, and her determination to look him in the eye and say thank you faltered.

'Yes?'

She swallowed. 'I just wanted to thank you. Properly. For...well...um...carrying me all that way.'

He grinned. 'I'm getting used to it. Although, if we're going to be doing that on a regular basis, I have to tell you that you could lose a little weight.'

'Oh, charming!' Actually, it felt a lot more real than some smooth, practised compliment of the 'light as a feather' variety. At least she knew he was telling the truth.

'Of course, if you're prepared to use your own two legs as transport, I'm quite prepared to admit that I think you're pretty much perfect just the way you are.'

She felt the heat rush to her face and hoped he'd put the pink cheeks down to the temperature. 'Apart from the combs,' she reminded him. She didn't want him getting too nice.

'Apart from the combs,' he agreed.

'And the blue toenails?'

'I've no objection to blue toenails.'

She wanted him to ask about them again, Bram realised. Wanted to share her own secrets. And he wanted to hear them. He wanted to know everything about Flora Claibourne. But not now. Not here.

He turned the Jeep on the narrow path and headed back to the coast.

They both breathed a little easier once they were back on the coast road, although Bram kept his thoughts to himself, his eyes on the road ahead. Flora too was quiet, concentrating on the view, the small sandy coves set amidst towering rock formations. On an impulse he turned off the road.

Flora threw a startled glance at him. 'Where are we going?'

'We're behind with our sightseeing. We can at least cross the beach picnic off the list.'

'No, Bram...' she objected as he got out and rounded the Jeep to open her door. She wasn't in the mood for a picnic any more. 'I need a shower. I have to wash off the jungle sweat.' Wash the creepy bat thing out of her hair.

'Try a swim instead,' he said, with a glance at the ocean, sparkling, bright, empty as far as the eye could see.

It was a lot closer than the hotel and it looked blissfully inviting, she thought, weakening.

Bram kicked off his shoes, stripped down to his underwear, then looked up. 'It isn't compulsory, but you might want to take off some of those clothes.'

She swallowed. 'Right.'

'Do you need a hand—'

'No! I can manage,' she said, and quickly began to unfasten the buttons of her shirt.

'—with your boots?' he finished. Grinning.

'I can manage,' she repeated stubbornly, through a mouth apparently stuffed with cotton wool.

He did it anyway, his wide shoulders spanning the open doorway as he bent to loosen her laces. She slipped out of her shirt, not sure whether she was pleased or disappointed to be wearing a wide-strapped sports bra that was quite as decent as any bikini top. Then, when he'd carefully eased off her boots, she lifted her bottom from the seat to shuck down her trousers. And winced as her knee brought her back to painful reality.

'This is a waste of time,' she said. 'There's no way I'm going to be able to walk across the sand. Or dive into the ocean. I'm sorry, Bram. It's a nice thought, but—' She stopped as he slid his hand beneath her knees. 'What are you doing?'

'Lean forward and put your arms around my neck.' She didn't move. 'Trust me, Flora. I'm your shadow, remember? We're inseparable.' And he lifted her into his arms and carried her down the beach and out into the sea.

Floating back in the cool water, her hair trailing behind her, and with Bram's hand firmly grasping hers, was as blissful as anything she could have imagined. Actually, her imagination didn't stretch that far.

'I'll say this for you, Bram Gifford, you certainly know how to pick a beach,' she said, by way of distraction. 'It has everything.' A perfect horseshoe of white sand, low palm trees bent to offer shade, a natural waterfall providing a fresh shower where the stream plunged over the rocks. 'This was a great idea,' she said.

'I have them occasionally.'

'Thank you for being so smart, Bram.'

'If I'd been smart, I'd have talked you out of the trip to the tomb.'

'No. That was good too,' she said. Especially the way he'd opened up, confided in her, trusted her. 'Apart from the bats.'

'Yes. It was. I'm glad I saw your princess.'

They drifted for a moment.

'She might have come here,' Flora said. 'Swum with the other maidens of the court in the early morning.'

'Or at night, with her lover.'

She heard herself sigh. 'I almost wish I wrote fiction so that I could invent an entire life for her. As it is, we'll probably never know who exactly she was and why she was buried there in such state.' She turned her face towards him. She hadn't expected him to be looking at her but he was, and for a moment the words froze in her throat. 'Thank you for being smart enough to stop me from going on my own, Bram. For being kind enough to come with me.'

'That's what shadows do. You can't go anywhere without me, remember?' And, as if to demonstrate the reality of that, he turned, scooped her back up into his arms and kicked for the shore.

'This is getting silly,' she said, as he stood up with her in the shallows and walked towards the natural shower. 'I've twisted my knee, not broken my leg.'

'I'm taking no chances,' he said, setting her down carefully beneath the spray. For a moment he continued to hold her against him, his skin warm against hers despite the sudden chill of the water, and she caught her breath.

'I owe you, Bram,' she said. 'I won't forget how much.'

'Does that mean I win this round of the Claibourne/ Farraday feud?'

She stared at him for a moment. She had forgotten all about the damn feud. 'Is that all you care about? Have you been taking notes of every stupid thing I've done today?' She stepped back without thinking and her knee buckled. His arm was around her waist before she could even register the pain.

'Why would I take notes?' he asked. 'Every moment of today is imprinted on my mind. Indelibly.'

Hers too, she thought. Hers too. But not for the same reasons. 'There's just one thing I don't understand.'

'Then ask, Bram,' she said carelessly. 'Anything.' After all, how much worse could it be?

'Anything?' he repeated, and without warning the mood shifted out of the sunlight into the shadows. Back to the darkness of the tomb and the moment when he'd bared his soul to her, trusted her with the deepest secret of his heart. And in the darkness she'd seen everything that—dazzled by his golden image—she had never been able to see in the daylight.

Bram Gifford was not some heartless philanderer who cared for nothing but his own pleasure. He was a work hard/play hard man who once, long ago, had fallen in love with a woman who'd used him. And he'd made sure he never made the same mistake again.

She owed him. He'd found the tomb for her. Carried her to safety when she'd fallen in her panic. Whatever he asked of her, whatever he wanted, she must tell him. And if he was simply using her, passing the hurt forward, well, she could take it. Maybe one day he'd recognise it for what it was. Unconditional love. And maybe it would finally set him free. Maybe it would finally set her free, too.

'Flora?' he murmured softly.

'What do you want to know?' she asked. And she held her breath, waiting for him to ask her to betray her sister.

CHAPTER TEN

'TELL me why you painted your toenails blue.'

Bram's question was so far from her own confused thoughts that for a moment Flora was sure she'd misheard him. 'I beg your pardon?'

'Your toenails. You don't paint your fingernails, yet you paint your toenails. Why?'

It took a moment for her heart to crank back into life, to slowly begin beating again. She was sharing a tropical paradise with a man who'd revealed himself to be everything she'd believed impossible. He'd been kind, tender, gentle. He hadn't uttered a single word of reproach for the mess she'd got him into. But of course that was all too good to be true.

He was a man, for heaven's sake. He'd expect some kind of payback. Not sex. He could have gone there last night—he'd been halfway there, for heaven's sake, and even though she'd been half expecting it she had no defence against him. But he hadn't been able to go through with it. Even with her hair loose.

Now she was in a situation where she owed him. She'd told him so. And he wanted information. But not about her sister. Or the store.

'My toenails? You want to know why I painted my toenails?'

'You were going to tell me when we were in town last night. We got sidetracked.'

'That's it?' she asked, still not sure where this was leading.

'Maybe.' Then, 'Depending on your answer, there may be a supplementary question.'

'Oh, right.'

For a moment she'd thought the world had been made over, just for her. It seemed she was mistaken. Instead of being her knight errant he was simply her shadow, adding up the mistakes, counting the errors. Well, she'd certainly made life easy for him.

The only unexplained phenomenon was her blue toenails. Last night it wouldn't have been a problem. She'd have told him and they might have laughed. Now she realised that it was a problem...

'Well?' he prompted, apparently impatient for her answer.

'It's nothing.'

He waited.

'It's silly, really. Nothing at all.'

'If it's nothing, tell me.'

'I can't... It's a secret pledge.'

'A secret pledge?'

Well, that had taken the smile right off his face. Except he hadn't actually been smiling. Only somewhere behind his eyes. And when he stopped it was like the lamps going out.

'Who with?'

'That's the supplementary question, right?'

'Who with?' he persisted.

She would have liked to spin out some fanciful yarn about a secret lover, a pledge of true love and a promise of love until death. Somehow, though, blue nail polish didn't quite live up to that scenario—and, anyway, he'd know she was lying. The hot pink flush would give her away in a heartbeat. And she wouldn't—couldn't lie to him. 'With my godson.'

He blinked. She'd surprised him. If she'd felt capable of feeling good about that, she'd have felt good. As it was…

'Why?' he asked.

'Does it matter?'

'Everything matters, Flora. I want to know everything about you.'

'Do you?' For a moment she felt a surge of something unexpected. Something that might have been joy. Then she realised that he was just being a Farraday, and that for the Farradays information was power. 'He's been picked for the football team at his school.'

'Football? It's May. He should be playing cricket.'

'He's seven, Bram. The bat would be bigger than him. And this is the big end of season match with their deadly rivals. I promised to be there to cheer him on and then this trip came up.'

'And how did painting the toenails help?'

'He said I had to do something so that he'd know I would be thinking of him—wear something in his school colours all the time.' She looked down, wiggled her toes. 'So I let him paint my toenails. He wanted to do one foot blue and the other yellow, but we compromised on the blue.'

'He made a pretty good job of it, for a seven-year-old.'

'I've touched them up a couple of times.' Please,

she thought, holding her breath. Please, please don't ask his name.

Almost as if he could read her mind, he said, 'What's his name?'

She hesitated a moment too long.

'John. His name is John, isn't it?'

She nodded.

'That's why you didn't want to tell me?'

She shrugged, turned away, stood beneath the spray to wash the salt from her skin, not wanting him to see how much she hadn't wanted to do or say anything that would hurt him.

'I'm going to need that supplementary question, Flora.'

'You've had your supplementary question. Twice.'

'That was all the same question. Now I want to know why you didn't paint your fingernails to match. Or any other colour. Who hurt you, Flora? What did he do to make you want to be invisible?'

'That's a hell of a supplementary question,' she muttered.

'They're the ones to watch out for,' he agreed, joining her under the spray, spreading out her hair, letting the water run through it.

Anything. He'd told her that she could ask him anything and he'd told her his deepest secrets, his darkest pain. She could do no less. 'Steve,' she said. 'His name was Steve.' She paused, thought about it. 'Still is, I guess.'

'Not Seb? Or Sam?'

She glanced uncertainly up at him, remembering

how she'd teased him, surprised that he remembered. 'Steve,' she repeated. 'I never forgot his name.'

'No, I didn't imagine for one minute that you had.'

'He was the most beautiful man I'd ever seen,' she said. *Bar one.* 'Thick corn-coloured hair, muscles like a professional tennis player. But then he had been a professional tennis player. My mother was between husbands that year and so she'd taken up tennis.' She turned away, lifting her face to the spray. 'It's a cliché, isn't it? Losing your virginity to the tennis coach.'

'Losing your virginity, however it happens, is always a cliché.'

'I was seventeen,' she said. 'Sweet seventeen and hardly ever been kissed. Not the way he could kiss, anyway. I threw myself at him shamelessly.'

'That's what your hormones demand when you're seventeen. It's nature's way of perpetuating the species.'

'I suppose it is.' She closed her eyes, feeling the sun on her face, the water pouring over her body.

'That's not all, is it?'

No. It wasn't all. 'I was into earrings in a big way then. Making them for my friends, making them for myself. I surpassed myself in an effort to catch his eye, make him notice me. Make him reach out and touch.'

'I doubt he needed that much encouragement.'

'Oh, he teased and flirted a little. But I wanted more. Much more.' She turned to face him, forcing him to let go of her hair, leaning back against the cold rock. 'The feather earrings were good. He tickled my neck with them. And a pair like little baby swings. They were toys, made to play with, and he didn't miss a beat. But it was the licorice allsorts that finally did it.'

'Licorice allsorts?'

'Big, bright and edible.' Bram said something brief and pretty much to the point. 'You've got it in one. He'd have had to be a saint to resist that much temptation.'

'I don't imagine he was that. And your mother? Where was she when all this was happening?'

'She was around. But she was busy. She spent hours at the beauty salon. Shopping. Keeping yourself looking that good is a full-time job, apparently. I never realised that he was hanging around for her. I thought I was the attraction. You have to realise that I was a very naïve seventeen-year-old.'

'Something he must have been very well aware of?'

'Maybe that was part of the attraction. There's nothing more tempting than forbidden fruit, and temptation was everywhere. In the summer house. In the dining room—'

'He had a resistance factor of zero, obviously.'

'Would that be a big turn-on for a man, do you think?' she asked. 'To have mother and daughter—?'

'I can't imagine it turning me on,' he said sharply. 'What happened when your mother found out?'

'She didn't. I was the one who found out. My mother took him to America with her for a week... Even then I didn't catch on. But when they came back they were married.'

'He's the toyboy she married?' He looked confused. 'I thought that was a fairly recent thing.'

'It is. Steve the tennis coach didn't last more than a few months. She's got a new model now.'

'What on earth did he say to you?'

'He didn't understand why I was so upset. He said he'd thought I knew, that I'd been doing it out of some sort of rebelliousness. He said he thought he was doing me a favour. He didn't see any reason why we shouldn't just carry on the way we were.'

'You told her?'

'My mother? No. I knew I'd been bad. Worse—I'd been stupid. Once I knew what had been going on, it all seemed so obvious. And I knew she'd be angrier with me than with him. He was a man, after all. What else could you expect?'

'A little more than that, I would have thought.'

'Yes, well, my father was her first husband and he set the trend for cheating on her. He was only faithful to India's mother. To be honest I don't think he ever got over her walking out on him.'

Bram made no comment and she sighed. 'What good would telling have done? It would just have made my mother unhappy sooner rather than later. So I went away to Italy for the summer on an art course, and by the time I came back he was history.'

'You never told anyone?'

'Only you.'

He reached out, touched her face with his fingers, and for a moment she thought he might kiss her. She couldn't bear the thought of him feeling sorry for her.

'Are you hungry?' she said quickly. She didn't wait for him to answer but turned and walked away, refusing to limp despite the pain in her knee.

'Your leg seems easier,' he said as he joined her at the Jeep.

'I guess the cold water helped,' she said, and despite the heat of the sun drying out her skin she shivered. She dried her hands and face on her shirt, then, as she went to put it back on over her damp bra, she saw the rip where Bram had stopped her headlong flight.

'Here,' he said, offering her his shirt. 'Wear this.'

'It'll get wet.'

'It doesn't matter. You'll burn.' She hesitated and he held it out for her, waited while she fed her arms into the long sleeves, then took his time about buttoning it up. He was too close, his sun-streaked hair flopping over his forehead as he bent to his task, brushing against her cheek.

'Thanks,' she said as he straightened. The word squeezed out from lungs that seemed deprived of oxygen. But he didn't let go, instead holding onto the collar, keeping her close.

'You should have told someone, Flora,' he said. 'India, perhaps. Or, if you couldn't talk to her, a counsellor. They'd have reassured you. Told you that you'd done nothing wrong.'

'I couldn't...' And yet she'd told him. Trusted him. As he'd trusted her.

'You don't have to hide from me, sweetheart. We're partners.' He kissed her forehead. 'No more secrets.' He kissed her mouth, soft and sweet, over almost before it had begun. 'And no more combs. Promise me.'

'I promise,' she whispered.

Bram's fingers tightened about the cloth, and for a moment the temptation was to take it further—much further. He wanted her so much. Wanted to show her that she was the most beautiful woman in the world. Second to no one. But why would she believe that he was any different? He was trying to take away something she took pride in, believed in, cared about.

He'd told her to trust him, but why should she? And what, when it came right down to it, did he know about her? They'd shared their secrets. He'd told her things that he'd thought he'd never tell another living soul. She'd laid open her heart. They'd come a long way in a very short time, but they both knew how easy it was to be deceived, made a fool of by desire.

For all her reserve, she'd come into his arms eagerly enough last night. And she was looking up at him now in a way that was calculated to heat a man's blood. His was hot enough to blow the top off a thermometer, but he took a mental and physical step back, distancing himself from what, a mere three days ago, would have seemed an impossibility. Distancing himself from the possibility of hurt.

'Right. Now we've got that sorted, let's have some lunch,' he said.

She looked as if he'd slapped her. Still. Shocked. Then she said, 'Actually, if you don't mind, I think I'd rather go back to the hotel. If I don't do something involving industrial quantities of conditioner to my hair very soon, I'll never get a comb through it again.'

It was an excuse, and they both knew it, but he opened the Jeep door without a word. The drive back was completed in almost total silence. As they walked into the hotel, though, they found themselves in the midst of a champagne celebration. Staff, guests—

everyone seemed to be partying. And in the midst of it all was the cool blonde, with Tipi Myan and a tall, thickset man—not unlike Bram to look at, Flora thought, but perhaps ten years older.

Tipi Myan detached himself from the group. 'Miss Claibourne! Mr Gifford! How good to see you enjoying yourselves. You've been to one of our beautiful beaches?'

'Amongst other things,' Bram said. 'What's the celebration?'

Dr Myan shrugged. 'There's no reason not to tell you now. I'm afraid that like many newly emerging nations we have a restless minority who wish to overthrow the established order—cause trouble.'

'And?'

'A small group intent on overthrowing our royal dynasty seized an engineer who came from Australia to look at the tomb and assess how best to make it quite safe. Protect it. They've been holding him hostage for the last five days.'

'What? Didn't it occur to you to stop Flora from coming here?' Bram demanded.

'It was too late, I'm afraid. By the time we realised what had happened, you were on your way. Of course you couldn't go to the tomb—'

'Been?' Flora interrupted. 'They've *been* holding him hostage? Past tense?'

'Yes, thank goodness. We rescued him this morning. Our security service mounted a dawn raid in the mountains, dealt with the rebels and brought him back to us safe and well. His poor wife has been so understanding. So patient... As you can imagine, the need for discretion—' He was distracted by an acquaintance.

'Poor woman,' Flora said. 'I was going to speak to her. I wish I had.' Then, glancing at Bram, she realised why he'd been avoiding her. 'She reminded you—' She stopped. 'I'm sorry.'

He covered her hand. 'You're right, of course, but I shouldn't assume everyone has a hidden agenda. I must try to be kinder.'

'I've got no complaints.'

'You are *too* kind,' he said with a wry smile as Tipi Myan rejoined them.

'I'm sorry…what was I saying?'

'Something about the need for discretion?' Bram suggested.

'It's always best if these things can be contained. But the good news is that it is now safe for you to go and see the tomb. Maybe tomorrow? There are amazing rock carvings that you will find enormously interesting, Dr Claibourne.'

'Actually, we've—' Flora began.

'I think Flora might prefer it if you just provided her with photographs,' Bram intervened swiftly, before she could confess. 'I don't want her taking any unnecessary risks. But we'll be at the museum first thing in the morning. Nine o'clock?'

Tipi Myan bowed his head. 'Of course. I'll be there.'

Bram grasped Flora's hand and led her away from the celebration. 'I don't think we need to tell Tipi Myan how we spent our morning, do you?'

'I'll never be able to keep it to myself.'

He shook his head. 'How on earth you kept your affair with the tennis coach a secret for so long defeats me.'

'Maybe it's because it was a one-off,' she admitted as he returned their cold box to Reception. 'Usually I'm hopeless at secrets.'

'You mean I won't have to torture you to find out what your sister has up her sleeve to keep the Farradays out of the store?'

'Torture me?'

'Tickling usually works,' he said, not quite smiling. 'But you clearly don't know anything or you'd have blurted it out by now.'

She immediately flushed bright pink.

'Miss Claibourne!' The receptionist greeted her with relief. 'I didn't expect you back until later. You have visitors.'

'Visitors?' she said, never taking her gaze from Bram's face.

The receptionist indicated a man and a young woman sitting quietly on a low sofa. 'They said you asked them to come here. I told them you would be late, but they insisted on waiting.'

'Right,' she said, but didn't move. They were still locked into the untold secret that her blush had betrayed. Bram stepped back. 'Whatever it is, I don't want to know.'

'But—'

'No.' He put his fingers to her lips, sealing them. 'Let's go and talk to your earring-maker.'

'That's your good deed for the day,' Bram said. The man who made the jewellery and his wife—who'd come along to translate—had gone beaming on their way, having arranged for Flora to visit his workshop. Bram was grinning too. 'You can send the hundred pounds you owe me to your favourite charity.'

'Consider it done.'

'Or you could take me out to dinner, instead?'

'I'm happy to do both, but we haven't actually had lunch yet,' she reminded him. They glanced towards the terrace, still noisy with celebration. 'I'm not dressed for company. I'll call Room Service,' she said, heading for the bungalow.

'Good plan.'

'And then I'll take a trip out to the weaving centre.'

'You can't drive with a bad knee.'

'Where I go, you go—isn't that what you said?' Then, a touch sarcastically, 'I'm sorry, would you prefer to take a siesta?'

'Only if that's an invitation.' Bram laughed as she blushed again. 'And I thought this was going to be dull. Go and fix your hair, Flora, while I order us some lunch, and then we'll go to see the weavers and the botanic gardens—'

'And pick up my jackets.'

'That too. Anywhere, in fact, where there are a lot of people.'

She frowned. 'You're looking for crowds?'

'We need to get to know one another a little better before…well, before we get to know one another a lot better.'

Flora fled for the shower before she changed her

mind about that siesta. But she left her hair loose and dressed with more care than she had in a long time.

Bram was signing the waiter's chit when Flora joined him on the veranda. Her hair hung loose and shining nearly to her waist and she was wearing a white shirt knotted casually beneath her breasts to offer a glimpse of her firm flat stomach. And she'd painted her fingernails to match her toes.

For a moment he came close to seizing her by the hand and forgetting all about lunch. But he resisted temptation, and as she sat opposite him at the small table, reached for a napkin, he said, 'Tell me your earliest memory.'

She stabbed a piece of ginger chicken salad with her fork. 'Gosh, this is good.' Then she glanced up and looked straight at him. 'This is your plan for us to get to know one another...better?'

'It's a start,' he said, his voice suddenly thick. He cleared his throat. 'I'll ask you a question, then it's your turn.'

'I can ask whatever I want?'

'Only the store is off limits.'

She shrugged. 'Okay. My earliest memory is my mother bending over me to kiss me goodnight. She was going out somewhere, I imagine, and she was wearing a necklace. I grabbed for it and it broke and the pearls went everywhere.'

'Was she angry?'

'No. She laughed, said I was a girl after her own heart.'

'Then she was wrong.'

'Was she? We both wanted, more than anything, to be loved. And you know what they say…' He waited for her to tell him. 'Women give sex to get love.'

'And men? What do they do?'

'Give love to get sex?'

About to tell her that she was wrong, it occurred to him that it was too easy to say the words. Flora needed a demonstration, not a declaration, so instead he said, 'It's your turn.'

'To ask a question?' She thought about it for a moment. 'Okay. Who was the first girl you kissed?'

'Sarah Carstairs,' he said, without hesitation. 'It was my first day at school. She knew where the pencils were kept and wouldn't tell me unless I kissed her.'

Flora laughed. 'What a hussy. How old was she?'

'Four. What is it they say in school reports? Must pay closer attention? If I'd been paying attention to the lesson she taught me that day I might have saved myself a lot of grief.'

'Hey, come on. Not all women are like that.'

'Nor are all men like Steve.'

She refused to meet his gaze. 'Have you finished?' she asked.

'Lunch or questions?'

'Lunch. We've got a lot to do this afternoon.'

'Will your leg stand it? I could do the tourist thing tomorrow while you're at the museum. Organise the cloth samples. Pick up your jackets, even.'

Apparently he'd said the right thing, because she reached out, took his hand. 'I want you to be with me when I see the princess's gold, Bram.' Then, her voice thick with a desire that neither of them were quite ready to acknowledge, she said, 'And meanwhile, if the knee plays up…' her lashes flickered as she lowered them '…I'll hold you to your promise to carry me.'

'Is that so?' He raised her fingers to his lips, brushing them over her freshly painted nails. 'So, Miss Claibourne, who's the hussy now?' he asked.

'Is that your next question?'

'Yes, but I'd advise you not to answer it. Not if you really want to go to the weaving centre.'

CHAPTER ELEVEN

THERE was a moment when anything might have happened. When they might have forgotten why they were in Saraminda, that they were on opposite sides in the battle for control of Claibourne & Farraday. When the past might have been brushed aside and only the future mattered.

Then she said, 'I really want to go the weaving centre.' And before he could respond Flora was on her feet and heading for the car park—more slowly than usual, to be sure, but still leaving him to follow or not, as he chose. Again.

'Hey,' he said, taking her arm so that she could lean on him, take the weight off her leg. 'We're a team, remember? You give the orders, I drive.'

She glanced up at him. 'Can you talk and drive at the same time?'

'We're back to the questions?'

'I didn't realise we'd ever left them.'

'In that case it's my turn.'

'You blew your turn, Bram.'

No. He'd done the right thing. Twice. Once last night. Once just now. Sex was the easy part. Trust, commitment, falling in love—they took something more, and neither of them were quite ready for that. 'So, what do you want to know?'

She paused for a moment, so that he was forced to

stop too. 'Everything,' she said. And then she moved on without waiting for his answer. 'What's your favourite food… No, scratch that. What *don't* you like?'

'Bananas,' he said. 'Cauliflower soup.'

She glanced at him. 'That's it?'

'Cottage cheese?' he offered.

'Oh, right,' she laughed. 'That's a match.'

'Coleslaw. And egg sandwiches…'

She pulled a face. 'The smell…'

They spent the rest of the afternoon catching up on the tourist sights. Flora organised a shipment of samples to be shipped back from the weaving centre to London. They wandered through the botanic gardens, wondering at the orchids and the hummingbirds and the butterflies.

They picked up her jackets from the tailor.

But all the time they continued swapping questions, occasionally laughing at the more ridiculous answers, on occasion moved almost to tears by an unexpectedly poignant response. The shared pain of the death of a favourite pet. The squirming anguish of embarrassments they'd rather forget. The scent of flowers on the grave of someone they'd loved.

They ate local fish in a small restaurant, then finally returned to their bungalow. 'Thank you for a lovely afternoon, Bram,' Flora said, turning in the doorway of her bedroom. 'A lovely day.'

'Apart from the bats.'

'It's a memory we share.'

'There'll be more of those.' Bram brushed her cheek with the lightest of kisses. 'I'll see you in the morning.' He didn't linger, but walked right along to his own room and shut the door.

He didn't leave it again, not even to walk on the beach, despite the fact that sleep eluded him for a long time.

He woke to a brassy sun and oppressive heat, and when they finally descended into the cool depths of the museum vault it was, despite the slightly claustrophobic weight of the stone walls closing in on them, almost a relief.

But the sight of the princess's treasure laid out, waiting for Flora, was enough to take his mind off his unease. It gleamed and shimmered in the bright overhead lighting. He had a feeling that it would gleam just as brightly in the dark.

'It's stunning,' he said, when Tipi Myan was called away and they were on their own. Flora nodded. She didn't touch anything, but stood and looked at it for a long time. 'Can I touch it?' She nodded and he carefully picked up the crown, held it for a moment, and then placed it on her head. 'I was right. You are the image of the princess.'

'No…'

'I want to see you in all this stuff…' Flora staggered slightly and he reached out to steady her. 'What the devil—?'

The floor beneath his feet seemed to ripple and they were showered with dust from the ceiling.

'A tremor…' And then there was no time for words. Instead he grabbed her, turning and pushing her away as part of the ceiling began to fall towards her. Then nothing.

'Bram! Bram, where are you? Please, answer me!' Flora crawled through the thick choking dust. And then she found him. Still, inert, a chunk of ceiling beside him. She wanted to scream. She wanted to cry.

But there was no time for that. Instead she put her head to his chest. Was there a heartbeat? She sought out his face in the dark, brushed the dust from his face, felt gently over his scalp for damage. Her fingers came away sticky with blood and she groaned.

He'd pushed her out of the way. It should have been her lying there with blood oozing from her head.

'Help!' She lifted her head and shouted, 'Is there anyone out there who can hear me?' Then, 'Bram... you just listen to me. You are not going to damn well die on me, do you hear? I won't allow it. I'll give you whatever you want...' She tried to find a pulse at his neck. Maybe she wasn't doing it right... It was one thing in the calm of a first aid lesson, quite another in the dark...

Calm. That was it. She had to keep calm. But all she wanted to do was shake him, make him wake up.

No. There it was. A pulse, strong and clear. So why wouldn't he wake up?

'Damn it, Bram. Wake up.' She grabbed at his shirt-front, bunching the cloth beneath her fingers. 'You can have it—do you hear? All of it. At least my part of the store. India will understand. At least, she won't, but I don't care.' Her voice rose in desperation. 'Listen to me! You wanted my secrets—well, I'm telling you one. She's going to wipe out the Farraday name. Change the name to Claibourne's. You don't want that, do you? I'll help you stop her, but you've got to come back to me.'

He groaned and she laid her head against his chest again. He was breathing; his heart was pumping. 'Just tell me what you want, my love. I'll do anything if only you'll come back. Give you anything. A son of your own to keep for ever—' Without warning he began to cough. 'Bram...'

'I'm here.' Then he groaned again. 'What does a man have to do to get the kiss of life around here?'

'Bram!' In her relief she flung herself at him, and he let out a sharp cry. 'What? Where are you hurt?'

He thought about it for a moment. 'Everywhere. What happened?'

'I think it was a tremor...' She too began to cough as the dust filled her throat. 'And like the chump you are you decided to be a hero instead of allowing nature to wipe out the opposition.'

'That doesn't sound like me.'

'Oh, sure. Mr Cynical. Just be still. I'll see if I can make someone hear.'

But he grabbed her arm. 'No. Don't go.'

'What is it? What can I do?'

'Just...'

'What?'

He reached up, touched the crown that was still, by some incredible chance, on her head. 'Tell me again, princess, how I can have it all...'

She swallowed, choking down the dust along with the bile of disappointment. He'd got everything he wanted, he seemed. 'It's yours,' she said. 'You've won.'

'Won?'

'Round two goes to the Farradays. A fair enough exchange for saving my life.' She touched his head. 'You could so easily have lost yours.'

'Flora—'

There was the sound of splintering wood and someone tried to prise open the door. She raised her voice. 'Can you hurry up, please? There's a man hurt in here.' Then she turned back to him. 'What is it, Bram?'

'When you said I could have it all, the only thing on my mind was you. And I might not be dying, but the kiss would be very welcome.'

He dozed most of the day and night and Flora never left him, eventually crawling into bed beside him when she nodded off herself and nearly fell off the bed.

'Flora?' She woke to find Bram propped on his elbow, looking down at her.

'Hi,' she said.

'Hi,' he said. Then, 'Tell me, princess, have I died and gone to heaven?'

'The doctor said I should keep an eye on you. Just in case of concussion.'

'Excellent doctor. What's the prognosis?'

'A few bumps and bruises. A grazed scalp. You'll live. How're you feeling?'

'You might not want to know the answer to that question.'

'You haven't got a headache, I take it?'

'Not one that I'm likely to notice. Hey, where are you going?' he demanded, as she threw back the covers and got out of bed. 'I need round-the-clock nursing.'

'Don't you want a drink? Something to eat?'

'I've got the only thing I want right here.'

'But—'

'Anything, you said. Anything I wanted.' And he rolled onto his back, grinning. 'You can start with a bed bath.'

'Forget it. There's nothing to stop you from using the shower.'

'I've had a knock on the head. I might get dizzy,' he pointed out.

'Then I guess I'll have to stay with you, just to make sure.'

'Flora…' He reached out, took her hand. 'You don't have to do that. You owe me nothing.'

'I owe you my life.'

'There are no debts in this relationship. We've come further in three days than some people do in a lifetime. We've shared our secrets, opened our hearts in a way that neither of us thought possible. When this is all over, whatever happens to the store, I want us to be partners. In every sense of the word.'

'You heard it all, didn't you?' she asked. 'You weren't unconscious.'

'Stunned,' he said. 'Momentarily. But you're right. I heard everything. At least I heard enough…'

'Faking it?'

'If I was pouring out my heart to you, would you

want to stop me?' She shook her head. 'You said you would give up the store if I recovered. I don't want that. I'm a lawyer, I can't replace you—can't feel what you feel, replace your enthusiasm.'

'It's odd, but a week ago I didn't understand what the store meant to me. Thought I didn't actually care... You've opened my eyes.'

'And yet you'd still give it up for me?'

'Yes,' she said. 'I'd give it up for you. I'd give you anything...'

'I know. I heard. But all I want is you. As for the store—why don't we leave it for India and Jordan to sort it out between them?' He swung his legs over the bed and stood up. 'We've got more important things to do.'

'Like what?' she whispered.

'First we'll take that shower,' he said. 'Then we'll make a start on "anything"...'

For all her bravado, Flora was trembling as she stepped into the shower with Bram, as the warm water sluiced over them both. This was new for her. A partnership of equals. Something she hadn't ever expected, hadn't ever believed possible.

'Would you like me to wash you?' she murmured.

He said nothing, just handed her a sponge, drizzled shower gel into it. Mouth dry, she began at his neck, washing him gently, carefully, kissing each of the bruises he'd sustained as he'd taken the rubble that should have fallen on her. Washing every bit of him. And then he took the sponge and did the same for her, not stopping even when her nipples tempted him and her skin flushed with obvious desire.

When his arousal became magnificently obvious.

'Bram.' She murmured his name, but still he took his time.

'There's no rush, my princess. We've got all the time in the world. The rest of our lives.'

'Time for something special?'

'Time for everything you ever wanted.'

She turned off the water, plucked a towel from the rack and, wrapping it around him, led him back to the bedroom.

She'd brought a huge wicker chair in from the living room to sit in and watch over him, but she led him past it, back to the bed. 'Sit there. Close your eyes and don't open them until I tell you.'

'Flora...'

'Shut,' she insisted, suddenly brilliantly confident. And Bram obeyed. His reward was the briefest touch of her lips against his, the soft teasing brush of her breasts against his chest. 'Keep them shut,' she repeated. 'Promise?'

'I promise.'

He heard her move away, her bare feet making no sound on the polished wood, and yet he knew he was alone. But he kept his word. And after a while he heard tiny noises. Tinkling, jingling noises. The soft squeak of the wicker as she sat down.

'Now you can open them.'

He'd known instinctively what she was doing, and yet the vision she presented was beyond imagining and for a moment he could not speak.

The diadem was on her head, just as it had been in the vault, the moment before the tremor. Her hair hung forward in tiny damp rippling waves over her naked breasts. Between them was a jade medallion set amidst row upon row of pearls.

Her arms were wound with gold and there were bangles at her ankles.

For a moment he couldn't speak. When he could he said, 'Promise me that the entire Saramindan police department isn't about to burst in here and arrest you.'

'They're copies, Bram. Tipi had already had them made for display in the tomb, when it's open to the public. I'm taking them back to London to put on display in the store.'

'You won't be wearing them?'

'No. This is a private show. One time only. Just for you.'

'I was right. You are my princess,' he said hoarsely. 'My Queen.' And he felt like a king as he took her hands and held her. Kissed her. Made her his.

The Royal Samarindan Botanical Gardens were alive with butterflies, the trees draped with wild orchids as Flora Claibourne and Bram Gifford made their marriage vows, quietly and without fuss.

'You're right about that look,' Bram said, as they toasted one another in champagne and cut the cake baked by Tipi Myan's wife while Tipi took photographs.

She was wearing deep blue and silver. Her jacket was made from the finest Saramindan cloth, her softly pleated trousers in fine billowing silk. They matched the dark blue polish on her finger and toenails. She'd been right about the high-heeled strappy sandals, too. And the earrings, made by a local craftswoman, were their names entwined in Saramindan script.

'It's going to be a hit.'

'There's only one problem left. How to tell Jordan and India that we've…um…merged,' Flora said.

'That's not a problem.'

'No?'

'No,' Bram said. 'Why bother them? They've both got far more important things on their minds.'

They exchanged a conspiratorial glance.

'That's true.'

'Jordan will start shadowing India in a day or two. And by the time we get back from our honeymoon it'll all be over.'

'We're going on honeymoon? It seems to me that we've been on honeymoon for weeks. I'll definitely be recommending Saraminda to the tourist department.'

'Honeymoon? My darling this wasn't a honeymoon. I've been shadowing you. Very closely. This was work.'

Flora laughed. 'I didn't realise how much I enjoyed being a director of Claibourne & Farraday. If Jordan wins, I shall hate having to give it up.'

'Then you have my word that you won't have to. You are a Farraday now…as well as a Claibourne. My name and my place on the board are my wedding gift to you.'

'That's an extraordinary wedding present.'

'You're an extraordinary woman. Believe me, they come with my heart, body and soul.' He paused beneath a sweetly scented trail of vanilla orchids to kiss her. 'Till death us do part.'

COMING
NEXT MONTH...

An exciting way to **save**
on the purchase of
Harlequin Romance® books!

Details to follow in July and August
Harlequin Romance books.

DON'T MISS IT!

HARLEQUIN®
Romance®

EMOTIONALLY EXHILARATING!

Contract Brides

A wedding dilemma:
What should a sexy, successful bachelor do if he's too
busy making millions to find a wife?

The perfect proposal:
The solution? For better, for worse, these grooms in a
hurry have decided to sign, seal and deliver the
ultimate marriage contract...to *buy* a bride!

Look out for these intensely emotional stories by some
of our most popular authors, beginning with:

Susan Fox
MARRIAGE ON DEMAND
(April 2002, #3696)

Also look out for thrilling marriage stories by
Margaret Way
and
Leigh Michaels

Coming soon in

*Harlequin
Romance*®

If you enjoyed what you just read,
then we've got an offer you can't resist!

Take 2 bestselling love stories FREE!

Plus get a FREE surprise gift!

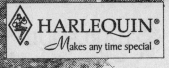

Harlequin Presents®
and
Harlequin Romance®
have come together to celebrate a year of royalty

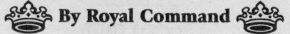 **By Royal Command**

 HARLEQUIN®
Romance®

EMOTIONALLY EXHILARATING!

Coming in June 2002
His Majesty's Marriage, #3703
Two original short stories by **Lucy Gordan** and **Rebecca Winters**

On-sale July 2002
The Prince's Proposal, #3709
by **Sophie Weston**

 HARLEQUIN®
Presents~

Seduction and Passion Guaranteed!

Coming in August 2002
Society Weddings, #2268
Two original short stories by **Sharon Kendrick** and **Kate Walker**

On-sale September 2002
The Prince's Pleasure, #2274
by **Robyn Donald**

**Escape into the exclusive world of royalty with
our royally themed books**

Available wherever Harlequin books are sold.

 HARLEQUIN®
Makes any time special ®